WHAT HAPPENED TO MIKE HAMMER?

For seven straight years he hit the bottle until he ended in the gutter. Seven years ago he sent a girl out on a job, a girl he loved. She never came back. That's when Mike Hammer started his fast skid to the bottom.

Then, from the lips of a dying man the alcoholic private eye got a shock that jolted his sodden nerves back to life.

Velda was alive! But not for long . . . unless Hammer could get to her quick.

Mike Hammer closes in on an underground network of international spies as he chases a mastermind assassin called the Dragon. They both want Velda, but the Dragon wants her dead. And there's someone who wants Hammer . . . that someone is a Spillane-special female, hauntingly bad, too beautiful to be good.

THE GIRL HUNTERS

by

Mickey Spillane

A SIGNET BOOK

Published by THE NEW AMERICAN LIBRARY

First Printing, March, 1963

Published as a SIGNET BOOK
by arrangement with E. P. Dutton and Company, Inc.,
who have authorized this softcover edition.
A hardcover edition is available from E. P. Dutton and
Company, Inc.

SIGNET TRADEMARK REG. U.S. PAT. OFF. AND FOREIGN COUNTRIES
REGISTERED TRADEMARK—MARCA REGISTRADA
HECHO EN CHICAGO, U.S.A.

SIGNET BOOKS are published by
The New American Library of World Literature, Inc.
501 Madison Avenue, New York 22, New York

PRINTED IN THE UNITED STATES OF AMERICA

This one is for Elliott Graham
who sweated more waiting for Mike
than he did as a dogface waiting for us
brown-shoes fly-boys to give him aerial cover.
So here we go again, E.G., with more to come. But
this one is for you.

THE
GIRL
HUNTERS

CHAPTER 1

They found me in the gutter. The night was the only thing I had left and not much of it at that. I heard the car stop, the doors open and shut and the two voices talking. A pair of arms jerked me to my feet and held me there.

"Drunk," the cop said.

The other one turned me around into the light. "He don't smell bad. That cut on his head didn't come from a fall either."

"Mugged?"

"Maybe."

I didn't give a damn which way they called it. They were both wrong anyhow. Two hours ago I was drunk. Not now. Two hours ago I was a roaring lion. Then the bottle sailed across the room. No lion left now.

Now was a time when I wasn't anything. Nothing was left inside except the feeling a ship must have when it's torpedoed, sinks and hits bottom.

A hand twisted into my chin and lifted my face up. "Ah, the guy's a bum. Somebody messed him up a little bit."

"You'll never make sergeant, son. That's a hundred-buck suit and it fits too good to be anything but his own. The dirt is fresh, not worn on."

"Okay, Daddy, let's check his wallet, see who he is and run him in."

The cop with the deep voice chuckled, patted me down and came up with my wallet. "Empty," he said.

Hell, there had been two bills in it when I started out. It must have been a pretty good night. Two hundred bucks' worth of night.

I heard the cop whistle between his teeth. "We got ourselves a real fish."

"Society boy? He don't look so good for a society boy. Not with his face. He's been splashed."

"Uh-uh. Michael Hammer, it says here on the card. He's a private jingle who gets around."

"So he gets tossed in the can and he won't get around so much."

The arm under mine hoisted me a little straighter and steered me toward the car. My feet moved; lumps on the end of a string that swung like pendulums.

"You're only joking," the cop said. "There are certain people who wouldn't like you to make such noises with your mouth."

"Like who?"

"Captain Chambers."

It was the other cop's turn to whistle.

"I told you this jingle was a fish," my pal said. "Go buzz the station. Ask what we should do with him. And use a phone—we don't want this on the air."

The cop grunted something and left. I felt hands easing me into the squad car, then shoving me upright against the seat. The hands went down and dragged my feet in, propping them against the floorboard. The door shut and the one on the other side opened. A heavy body climbed in under the wheel and a tendril of smoke drifted across my face. It made me feel a little sick.

The other cop came back and got in beside me. "The captain wants us to take him up to his house," he said. "He told me thanks."

"Good enough. A favor to a captain is like money in the bank, I always say."

"Then how come you ain't wearing plainclothes then?"

"Maybe I'm not the type, son. I'll leave it to you young guys."

The car started up. I tried to open my eyes but it took too much effort and I let them stay closed.

You can stay dead only so long. Where first there was nothing, the pieces all come drifting back together like a movie of an exploding shell run in reverse. The fragments come back slowly, grating together as they seek a matching part and painfully jar into place. You're whole again, finally, but the scars and the worn places are all there to remind you that once you were dead. There's life once more and, with it, a dull pain that pulsates at regular intervals, a light that's too bright to look into and sound that's more than you can stand. The flesh is weak and crawly, slack from the disuse that is the death, sensitive with the agonizing fire that is life. There's memory that makes you want to crawl back into the void but the life is too vital to let you go.

The terrible shattered feeling was inside me, the pieces having a hard time trying to come together. My throat was still raw and cottony; constricted, somehow, from the tensed-up muscles at the back of my neck.

"When I looked up Pat was holding out his cigarettes to me. "Smoke?"

I shook my head.

His voice had a callous edge to it when he said, "You quit?"

"Yeah."

I felt his shrug. "When?"

"When I ran out of loot. Now knock it off."

"You had loot enough to drink with." His voice had a real dirty tone now.

There are times when you can't take anything at all, no jokes, no rubs—nothing. Like the man said, you want nothing from nobody never. I propped my hands on the arms of the chair and pushed myself to my feet. The inside of my thighs quivered with the effort.

"Pat—I don't know what the hell you're pulling. I don't give a damn either. Whatever it is, I don't appreciate it. Just keep off my back, old buddy."

A flat expression drifted across his face before the hardness came back. "We stopped being buddies a long time ago, Mike."

"Good. Let's keep it like that. Now where the hell's my clothes?"

He spit a stream of smoke at my face and if I didn't have to hold the back of the chair to stand up I would have belted him one. "In the garbage," he said. "It's where you belong too but this time you're lucky."

"You son of a bitch."

I got another faceful of smoke and choked on it.

"You used to look a lot bigger to me, Mike. Once I couldn't have taken you. But now you call me things like that and I'll belt you silly."

"You son of a bitch," I said.

I saw it coming but couldn't move, a blurred white open-handed smash that took me right off my feet into the chair that turned over and left me in a sprawled lump against the wall. There was no pain to it, just a taut sickness in the belly that turned into a wrenching dry heave that tasted of blood from the cut inside my mouth. I could feel myself twitching spasmodically with every contraction of my stomach and when it was over I lay there with relief so great I thought I was dead.

He let me get up by myself and half fall into the chair. When I could focus again, I said, "Thanks, buddy. I'll keep it in mind."

Pat shrugged noncommittally and held out a glass. "Water. It'll settle your stomach."

"Drop dead."

He put the glass down on an end table as the bell rang. When he came back he threw a box down on the sofa and pointed to it. "New clothes. Get dressed."

"I don't have any new clothes."

"You have now. You can pay me later."

"I'll pay you up the guzukus later."

He walked over, seemingly balancing on the balls of his feet. Very quietly he said, "You can get yourself another belt in the kisser without trying hard, mister."

I couldn't let it go. I tried to swing coming up out of the chair and like the last time I could see it coming but couldn't get out of the way. All I heard was a meaty smash that had a familiar sound to it and my stomach tried to heave again but it was too late. The beautiful black had come again.

My jaws hurt. My neck hurt. My whole side felt like it was coming out. But most of all my jaws hurt. Each tooth was an independent source of silent agony while the pain in my head seemed to center just behind each ear. My tongue was too thick to talk and when I got my eyes open I had to squint them shut again to make out the checkerboard pattern of the ceiling.

When the fuzziness went away I sat up, trying to remember what happened. I was on the couch this time, dressed in a navy blue suit. The shirt was clean and white, the top button open and the black knitted tie hanging down loose. Even the shoes were new and in the open part of my mind it was like the simple wonder of a child discovering the new and strange world of the ants when he turns over a rock.

"You awake?"

I looked up and Pat was standing in the archway, another guy behind him carrying a small black bag.

When I didn't answer Pat said, "Take a look at him, Larry."

The one he spoke to pulled a stethoscope from his pocket and hung it around his neck. Then everything started coming back again. I said, "I'm all right. You don't hit that hard."

"I wasn't half trying, wise guy."

"Then why the medic?"

"General principles. This is Larry Snyder. He's a friend of mine."

"So what?" The doc had the stethoscope against my chest but I couldn't stop him even if I had wanted to. The examination was quick, but pretty thorough. When he finished he stood up and pulled out a prescription pad.

Pat asked, "Well?"

"He's been around. Fairly well marked out. Fist fights, couple of bullet scars—"

"He's had them."

"Fist marks are recent. Other bruises made by some blunt instrument. One rib—"

"Shoes," I interrupted. "I got stomped."

"Typical alcoholic condition," he continued. "From all external signs I'd say he isn't too far from total. You know how they are."

"Damn it," I said, "quit talking about me in the third person."

Pat grunted something under his breath and turned to Larry. "Any suggestions?"

"What can you do with them?" the doctor laughed. "They hit the road again as soon as you let them out of your sight. Like him—you buy him new clothes and as soon as he's near a swap shop he'll turn them in on rags with cash to boot and pitch a big one. They go back harder than ever once they're off awhile."

"Meanwhile I can cool him for a day."

"Sure. He's okay now. Depends upon personal supervision."

Pat let out a terse laugh. "I don't care what he does when I let him loose. I want him sober for one hour. I need him."

When I glanced up I saw the doctor looking at Pat strangely, then me. "Wait a minute. This is that guy you were telling me about one time?"

Pat nodded. "That's right."

"I thought you were friends."

"We were at one time, but nobody's friends with a damn drunken bum. He's nothing but a lousy lush and I'd as soon throw his can in the tank as I would any other lush. Being friends once doesn't mean anything to me. Friends can wear out pretty fast sometimes. He wore out. Now he's part of a job. For old times' sake I throw in a few favors on the side but they're strictly for old times' sake and only happen once. Just once. After that he stays bum and I stay cop. I catch him out of line and he's had it."

Larry laughed gently and patted him on the shoulder. Pat's face was all tight in a mean grimace and it was a way I had never seen him before. "Relax," Larry told him. "Don't *you* get wound up."

"So I hate slobs," he said.

"You want a prescription too? There are economy-sized bottles of tranquilizers nowadays."

Pat sucked in his breath and a grin pulled at his mouth. "That's all I need is a problem." He waved a thumb at me. "Like him."

Larry looked down at me like he would at any specimen. "He doesn't look like a problem type. He probably plain likes the sauce."

"No, he's got a problem, right?"

"Shut up," I said.

"Tell the man what your problem is, Mikey boy."

Larry said, "Pat—"

He shoved his hand away from his arm. "No, go ahead and tell him, Mike. I'd like to hear it again myself."

"You son of a bitch," I said.

He smiled then. His teeth were shiny and white under tight lips and the two steps he took toward me were stiff-kneed. "I told you what I'd do if you got big-mouthed again."

For once I was ready. I wasn't able to get up, so I kicked him right smack in the crotch and once in the mouth when he started to fold up and I would have gotten one more in if the damn doctor hadn't laid me out with a single swipe of his bag that almost took my head off.

It was an hour before either one of us was any good, but from now on I wasn't going to get another chance to lay Pat up with a sucker trick. He was waiting for me to try it and if I did he'd have my guts all over the floor.

The doctor had gone and come, getting his own prescriptions filled. I got two pills and a shot. Pat had a fistful of

aspirins, but he needed a couple of leeches along the side
of his face where he was all black and blue.

But yet he sat there with the disgust and sarcasm still
on his face whenever he looked at me and once more he
said, "You didn't tell the doctor your problem, Mike."

I just looked at him.

Larry waved his hand for him to cut it out and finished
repacking his kit.

Pat wasn't going to let it alone, though. He said, "Mike
lost his girl. A real nice kid. They were going to get married."

That great big place in my chest started to open up
again, a huge hole that could grow until there was nothing
left of me, only that huge hole. "Shut up, Pat."

"He likes to think she ran off, but he knows all the time
she's dead. He sent her out on too hot a job and she never
came back, right, Mikey boy? She's dead."

"Maybe you'd better forget it, Pat," Larry told him
softly.

"Why forget it? She was my friend too. She had no
business playing guns with hoods. But no, wise guy here
sends her out. His secretary. She has a P.I. ticket and a
gun, but she's nothing but a girl and she never comes
back. You know where she probably is, Doc? At the bottom of the river someplace, that's where."

And now the hole was all I had left. I was all nothing,
a hole that could twist and scorch my mind with such
incredible pain that even relief was inconceivable because
there was no room for anything except that pain. Out of
it all I could feel some movement. I knew I was watching
Pat and I could hear his voice but nothing made sense at
all.

His voice was far away saying, "Look at him, Larry. His
eyes are all gone. And look at his hand. You know what
he's doing. He's trying to kill me. He's going after a gun
that isn't there anymore because he hasn't got a license
to carry one. He lost that and his business and everything
else when he shot up the people he thought got Velda.
Oh, he knocked off some goodies and got away with it

because they were all hoods caught in the middle of an armed robbery. But that was it for our tough boy there. Then what does he do? He cries his soul out into a whiskey bottle. Damn—look at his hand. He's pointing a gun at me he doesn't even have anymore and his finger's pulling the trigger. Damn, he'd kill me right where I sit."

Then I lost sight of Pat entirely because my head was going from side to side and the hole was being filled in again from the doctor's wide-fingered slaps until once more I could see and feel as much as I could in the half life that was left in me.

This time the doctor had lost his disdainful smirk. He pulled the skin down under my eyes, stared at my pupils, felt my pulse and did things to my earlobe with his finger-nail that I could barely feel. He stopped, stood up and turned his back to me. "This guy is shot down, Pat."

"It couldn't've happened to a better guy."

"I'm not kidding. He's a case. What do you expect to get out of him?"

"Nothing. Why?"

"Because I'd say he couldn't stay rational. That little exhibition was a beauty. I'd hate to see it if he was pressed further."

"Then stick around. I'll press him good, the punk."

"You're asking for trouble. Somebody like him can go off the deep end anytime. For a minute there I thought he'd flipped. When it happens they don't come back very easily. What is it you wanted him to do?"

I was listening now. Not because I wanted to, but because it was something buried too far in my nature to ignore. It was something from away back like a hunger that can't be ignored.

Pat said, "I want him to interrogate a prisoner."

For a moment there was silence, then: "You can't be serious."

"The hell I'm not. The guy won't talk to anybody else *but* him."

"Come off it, Pat. You have ways to make a person talk."

"Sure, under the right circumstances, but not when they're in the hospital with doctors and nurses hovering over them."

"Oh?"

"The guy's been shot. He's only holding on so he can talk to this slob. The doctors can't say what keeps him alive except his determination to make this contact."

"But—"

"But nuts, Larry!" His voice started to rise with suppressed rage. "We use any means we can when the chips are down. This guy was shot and we want the one who pulled the trigger. It's going to be a murder rap any minute and if there's a lead we'll damn well get it. I don't care what it takes to make this punk sober, but that's the way he's going to be and I don't care if the effort kills him, he's going to do it."

"Okay, Pat. It's your show. Run it. Just remember that there are plenty of ways of killing a guy."

I felt Pat's eyes reach out for me. "For him I don't give a damn."

Somehow I managed a grin and felt around for the words. I couldn't get a real punch line across, but to me they sounded good enough.

Just two words.

CHAPTER 2

Pat had arranged everything with his usual methodical care. The years hadn't changed him a bit. The great arranger. Mr. Go, Go, Go himself. I felt the silly grin come back that really had no meaning, and someplace in the back of my mind a clinical voice told me softly that it could be a symptom of incipient hysteria. The grin got sillier and I couldn't help it.

Larry and Pat blocked me in on either side, a hand under each arm keeping me upright and forcing me forward. As far as anybody was concerned I was another sick one coming in the emergency entrance and if he looked close enough he could even smell the hundred-proof sickness.

I made them take me to the men's room so I could vomit again, and when I sluiced down in frigid water I felt a small bit better. Enough so I could wipe off the grin. I was glad there was no mirror over the basin. It had been a long time since I had looked at myself and I didn't want to start now.

Behind me the door opened and there was some hurried medical chatter between Larry and a white-coated intern who had come in with a plainclothesman. Pat finally said, "How is he?"

19

"Going fast," Larry said. "He won't let them operate either. He knows he's had it and doesn't want to die under ether before he sees your friend here."

"Damn it, don't call him my friend."

The intern glanced at me critically, running his eyes up and down then doing a quickie around my face. His fingers flicked out to spread my eyelids open for a look into my pupils and I batted them away.

"Keep your hands off me, sonny," I said.

Pat waved him down. "Let him be miserable, Doctor. Don't try to help him."

The intern shrugged, but kept looking anyway. I had suddenly become an interesting psychological study for him.

"You'd better get him up there. The guy hasn't long to live. Minutes at the most."

Pat looked at me. "You ready?"

"You asking?" I said.

"Not really. You don't have a choice."

"No?"

Larry said, "Mike—go ahead and do it."

I nodded. "Sure, why not. I always did have to do half his work for him anyway." Pat's mouth went tight and I grinned again. "Clue me on what you want to know."

There were fine white lines around Pat's nostrils and his lips were tight and thin. "Who shot him. Ask him that."

"What's the connection?"

Now Pat's eyes went half closed, hating my guts for beginning to think again. After a moment he said, "One bullet almost went through him. They took it out yesterday. A ballistics check showed it to be from the same gun that killed Senator Knapp. If this punk upstairs dies we can lose our lead to a murderer. Understand? You find out who shot him."

"Okay," I said. "Anything for a friend. Only first I want a drink."

"No drink."

"So drop dead."

"Bring him a shot," Larry told the intern.

The guy nodded, went out and came back a few seconds later with a big double in a water glass. I took it in a hand that had the shakes real bad, lifted it and said, "Cheers."

The guy on the bed heard us come in and turned his head on the pillow. His face was drawn, pinched with pain and the early glaze of death was in his eyes.

I stepped forward and before I could talk he said, "Mike? You're—Mike Hammer?"

"That's right."

He squinted at me, hesitating. "You're not like—"

I knew what he was thinking. I said, "I've been sick."

From someplace in back Pat sucked in his breath disgustedly.

The guy noticed them for the first time. "Out. Get them out."

I waved my thumb over my shoulder without turning around. I knew Larry was pushing Pat out the door over his whispered protestations, but you don't argue long with a medic in his own hospital.

When the door clicked shut I said, "Okay, buddy, you wanted to see me and since you're on the way out it has to be important. Just let me get some facts straight. I never saw you before. Who are you?"

"Richie Cole."

"Good. Now who shot you?"

"Guy they call . . . The Dragon. No name . . . I don't know his name."

"Look . . ."

Somehow he got one hand up and waved it feebly. "Let me talk."

I nodded, pulled up a chair and sat on the arm. My guts were all knotted up again and beginning to hurt. They were crying out for some bottle love again and I had to rub the back of my hand across my mouth to take the thought away.

The guy made a wry face and shook his head. "You'll . . . never do it."

My tongue ran over my lips without moistening them. "Do what?"

"Get her in time."

"Who?"

"The woman." His eyes closed and for a moment his face relaxed. "The woman Velda."

I sat there as if I were paralyzed; for a second totally immobilized, a suddenly frozen mind and body that had solidified into one great silent scream at the mention of a name I had long ago consigned to a grave somewhere. Then the terrible cold was drenched with an even more terrible wash of heat and I sat there with my hands bunched into fists to keep them from shaking.

Velda.

He was watching me closely, the glaze in his eyes momentarily gone. He saw what had happened to me when he said the name and there was a peculiar expression of approval in his face.

Finally I said, "You knew her?"

He barely nodded. "I *know* her."

And again that feeling happened to me, worse this time because I knew he wasn't lying and that she was alive someplace. *Alive!*

I kept a deliberate control over my voice. "Where is she?"

"Safe for . . . the moment. But she'll be killed unless . . . you find her. The one called The Dragon . . . he's looking for her too. You'll have to find her first."

I was damn near breathless. *"Where?"* I wanted to reach over and shake it out of him but he was too close to the edge of the big night to touch.

Cole managed a crooked smile. He was having a hard time to talk and it was almost over. "I gave . . . an envelope to Old Dewey. Newsy on Lexington by the Clover Bar . . . for you."

"Damn it, where is she, Cole?"

"No . . . you find The Dragon . . . before he gets her."

"Why me, Cole? Why that way? You had the cops?"

The smile still held on. "Need someone . . . ruthless. Someone very terrible." His eyes fixed on mine, shiny bright, mirroring one last effort to stay alive. "She said . . .

you could . . . if someone could find you. You had been missing . . . long time." He was fighting hard now. He only had seconds. "No police . . . unless necessary. You'll see . . . why."

"Cole . . ."

His eyes closed, then opened and he said, "Hurry." He never closed them again. The gray film came and his stare was a lifeless one, hiding things I would have given an arm to know.

I sat there beside the bed looking at the dead man, my thoughts groping for a hold in a brain still soggy from too many bouts in too many bars. I couldn't think, so I simply looked and wondered where and when someone like him had found someone like her.

Cole had been a big man. His face, relaxed in death, had hard planes to it, a solid jaw line blue with beard and a nose that had been broken high on the bridge. There was a scar beside one eye running into the hairline that could have been made by a knife. Cole had been a hard man, all right. In a way a good-looking hardcase whose business was trouble.

His hand lay outside the sheet, the fingers big and the wrist thick. The knuckles were scarred, but none of the scars was fresh. They were old scars from old fights. The incongruous part was the nails. They were thick and square, but well cared for. They reflected all the care a manicurist could give with a treatment once a week.

The door opened and Pat and Larry came in. Together they looked at the body and stood there waiting. Then they looked at me and whatever they saw made them both go expressionless at once.

Larry made a brief inspection of the body on the bed, picked up a phone and relayed the message to someone on the other end. Within seconds another doctor was there with a pair of nurses verifying the situation, recording it all on a clipboard.

When he turned around he stared at me with a peculiar expression and said, "You feel all right?"

"I'm all right," I repeated. My voice seemed to come from someone else.

"Want another drink?"

"No."

"You'd better have one," Larry said.

"I don't want it."

Pat said, "The hell with him." His fingers slid under my arm. "Outside, Mike. Let's go outside and talk."

I wanted to tell him what he could do with his talk, but the numbness was there still, a frozen feeling that restricted thought and movement, painless but effective. So I let him steer me to the small waiting room down the hall and took the seat he pointed out.

There is no way to describe the immediate aftermath of a sudden shock. If it had come at another time in another year it would have been different, but now the stalk of despondency was withered and brittle, refusing to bend before a wind of elation.

All I could do was sit there, bringing back his words, the tone of his voice, the way his face crinkled as he saw me. Somehow he had expected something different. He wasn't looking for a guy who had the earmarks of the Bowery and every slop chute along the avenues etched into his skin.

I said, "Who was he, Pat?" in a voice soggy and hollow.

Pat didn't bother to answer my question. I could feel his eyes crawl over me until he asked, "What did he tell you?"

I shook my head. Just once. My way could be final too.

With a calm, indifferent sincerity Pat said, "You'll tell me. You'll get worked on until talking won't even be an effort. It will come out of you because there won't be a nerve ending left to stop it. You know that."

I heard Larry's strained voice say, "Come off it, Pat. He can't take much."

"Who cares. He's no good to anybody. He's a louse, a stinking, drinking louse. Now he's got something I have to have. You think I'm going to worry about him? Larry, buddy, you just don't know me very well anymore."

I said, "Who was he?"

The wall in front of me was a friendly pale green. It was blank from one end to the other. It was a vast, meadowlike area, totally unspoiled. There were no foreign markings, no distracting pictures. Unsympathetic. Antiseptic.

I felt Pat's shrug and his fingers bit into my arm once more. "Okay, wise guy. Now we'll do it my way."

"I told you, Pat—"

"Damn it, Larry, you knock it off. This bum is a lead to a killer. He learned something from that guy and I'm going to get it out of him. Don't hand me any pious crap or medical junk about what can happen. I know guys like this. I've been dealing with them all my life. They go on getting banged around from saloon to saloon, hit by cars, rolled by muggers and all they ever come up with are fresh scars. I can beat hell out of him and maybe he'll talk. Maybe he won't, but man, let me tell you this—I'm going to have my crack at him and when I'm through the medics can pick up the pieces for their go. Only first me, understand?"

Larry didn't answer him for a moment, then he said quietly. "Sure, I understand. Maybe you could use a little medical help yourself."

I heard Pat's breath hiss in softly. Like a snake. His hand relaxed on my arm and without looking I knew what his face was like. I had seen him go like that before and a second later he had shot a guy.

And this time it was me he listened to when I said, "He's right, old buddy. You're real sick."

I knew it would come and there wouldn't be any way of getting away from it. It was quick, it was hard, but it didn't hurt a bit. It was like flying away to never-never land where all is quiet and peaceful and awakening is under protest because then it will really hurt and you don't want that to happen.

Larry said, "How do you feel now?"

It was a silly question. I closed my eyes again.

"We kept you here in the hospital."

"Don't do me any more favors," I told him.

"No trouble. You're a public charge. You're on the books as an acute alcoholic with a D and D to boot and if you're real careful you might talk your way out on the street again. However, I have my doubts about it. Captain Chambers is pushing you hard."

"The hell with him."

"He's not the only one."

"So what's new?" My voice was raspy, almost gone.

"The D.A., his assistant and some unidentified personnel from higher headquarters are interested in whatever statement you'd care to make."

"The hell with them too."

"It could be instrumental in getting you out of here."

"Nuts. It's the first time I've been to bed in a long time. I like it here."

"Mike—" His voice had changed. There was something there now that wasn't that of the professional medic at a bedside. It was worried and urgent and I let my eyes slit open and looked at him.

"I don't like what's happening to Pat."

"Tough."

"A good word, but don't apply it to him. You're the tough one. You're not like him at all."

"He's tough."

"In a sense. He's a pro. He's been trained and can perform certain skills most men can't. He's a policeman and most men aren't that. Pat is a normal sensitive human. At least he was. I met him after you went to pot. I heard a lot about you, mister. I watched Pat change character day by day and what caused the change was you and what you did to Velda."

The name again. In one second I lived every day the name was alive and with me. Big, Valkyrian and with hair as black as night.

"Why should he care?"

"He says she was his friend."

Very slowly I squeezed my eyes open. "You know what she was to me?"

"I think so."

"Okay."

"But it could be he was in love with her too," he said.

I couldn't laugh like I wanted to. "She was in love with me, Doc."

"Nevertheless, *he* was in love with *her*. Maybe you never realized it, but that's the impression I got. He's still a bachelor, you know."

"Ah! He's in love with his job. I know him."

"Do you?"

I thought back to that night ago and couldn't help the grin that tried to climb up my face. "Maybe not, Doc, maybe not. But it's an interesting thought. It explains a lot of things."

"He's after you now. To him, you killed her. His whole personality, his entire character has changed. You're the focal point. Until now he's never had a way to get to you to make you pay for what happened. Now he has you in a nice tight bind and, believe me, you're going to be racked back first class."

"That's G.I. talk, Doc."

"I was in the same war, buddy."

I looked at him again. His face was drawn, his eyes searching and serious. "What am I supposed to do?"

"He never told me and I never bothered to push the issue, but since I'm his friend rather than yours, I'm more interested in him personally than you."

"Lousy bedside manner, Doc."

"Maybe so, but he's my friend."

"He used to be mine."

"No more."

"So?"

"What happened?"

"What would you believe coming from an acute alcoholic and a D and D?"

For the first time he laughed and it was for real. "I hear you used to weigh in at two-o-five?"

"Thereabouts."

"You're down to one-sixty-eight, dehydrated, under-nourished. A bum, you know?"

"You don't have to remind me."

"That isn't the point. You missed it."

"No I didn't."

"Oh?"

"Medics don't talk seriously to D and D's. I know what I was. Now *there* is a choice of words if you can figure it out."

He laughed again. "*Was.* I caught it."

"Then talk."

"Okay. You're a loused-up character. There's nothing to you anymore. Physically, I mean. Something happened and you tried to drink yourself down the drain."

"I'm a weak person."

"Guilt complex. Something you couldn't handle. It happens to the hardest nuts I've seen. They can take care of anything until the irrevocable happens and then they blow. Completely."

"Like me?"

"Like you."

"Keep talking."

"You were a lush."

"So are a lot of people. I even know some doctors who —"

"You came out of it pretty fast."

"At ease, Doc."

"I'm not prying," he reminded me.

"Then talk right."

"Sure," he said. "Tell me about Velda."

CHAPTER 3

"It was a long time ago," I said.

And when I had said it I wished I hadn't because it was something I never wanted to speak about. It was over. You can't beat time. Let the dead stay dead. If they can. But was she dead? Maybe if I told it just once I could be sure.

"Tell me," Larry asked.

"Pat ever say anything?"

"Nothing."

So I told him.

"It was a routine job," I said.

"Yes?"

"A Mr. Rudolph Civac contacted me. He was from Chicago, had plenty of rocks and married a widow named Marta Singleton who inherited some kind of machine-manufacturing fortune. Real social in Chicago. Anyway, they came to New York where she wanted to be social too and introduce her new husband around."

"Typical," Larry said.

"Rich-bitches."

"Don't hold it against them," he told me.

"Not me, kid," I said.

"Then go on."

I said, "She was going to sport all the gems her dead

husband gave her which were considerable and a prime target for anybody in the field and her husband wanted protection."

Larry made a motion with his hand. "A natural thought."

"Sure. So he brought me in. Big party. He wanted to cover the gems."

"Any special reason?"

"Don't be a jerk. They were worth a half a million. Most of my business is made of stuff like that."

"Trivialities."

"Sure, Doc, like unnecessary appendectomies."

"Touché."

"Think nothing of it."

He stopped then. He waited seconds and seconds and watched and waited, then: "A peculiar attitude."

"You're the psychologist, Doc, not me."

"Why?"

"You're thinking that frivolity is peculiar for a D and D."

"So go on with the story."

"Doc," I said, "later I'm going to paste you right in the mouth. You know this?"

"Sure."

"That's *my* word."

"So sure."

"Okay, Doc, ask for it. Anyway, it was a routine job. The target was a dame. At that time a lot of parties were being tapped by a fat squad who saw loot going to waste around the neck of a big broad who never needed it—but this was a classic. At least in our business."

"How?"

"Never mind. At least she called us in. I figured it would be better if we changed our routine. That night I was on a homicide case. Strictly insurance, but the company was paying off and there would be another grand in the kitty. I figured it would be a better move to let Velda cover the affair since she'd be able to stay with the client at all times, even into the ladies' room."

Larry interrupted with a wave of his hand. "Mind a rough question?"

"No."

"Was this angle important or were you thinking, rather, of the profit end—like splitting your team up between two cases."

I knew I had started to shake and pressed my hands against my sides hard. After a few seconds the shakes went away and I could answer him without wanting to tear his head off. "It was an important angle," I said. "I had two heists pulled under my nose when they happened in a powder room."

"And—the woman. How did she feel about it?"

"Velda was a pro. She carried a gun and had her own P.I. ticket."

"And she could handle any situation?"

I nodded. "Any we presumed could happen here."

"You were a little too presumptuous, weren't you?"

The words almost choked me when I said, "You know, Doc, you're asking to get killed."

He shook his head and grinned. "Not you, Mike. You aren't like you used to be. I could take you just as easy as Pat did. Almost anybody could."

I tried to get up, but he laid a hand on my chest and shoved me back and I couldn't fight against him. Every nerve in me started to jangle and my head turned into one big round blob of pain.

Larry said, "You want a drink?"

"No."

"You'd better have one."

"Stuff it."

"All right, suffer. You want to talk some more or shall I take off?"

"I'll finish the story. Then you can work on Pat. When I get out of here I'm going to make a project of rapping you and Pat right in the mouth."

"Good. You have something to look forward to. Now talk."

I waited a minute, thinking back years and putting the

pieces in slots so familiar they were worn smooth at the edges. Finally I said, "At eleven o'clock Velda called me at a prearranged number. Everything was going smoothly. There was nothing unusual, the guests were all persons of character and money, there were no suspicious or unknown persons present including the household staff. At that time they were holding dinner awaiting the arrival of Mr. Rudolph Civac. That was my last connection with Velda."

"There was a police report?"

"Sure. At 11:15 Mr. Civac came in and after saying hello to the guests, went upstairs with his wife for a minute to wash up. Velda went along. When they didn't appear an hour and a half later a maid went up to see if anything was wrong and found the place empty. She didn't call the police, thinking that they had argued or something, then went out the private entrance to the rear of the estate. She served dinner with a lame excuse for the host's absence, sent the guests home and cleaned up with the others.

"The next day Marta Civac was found in the river, shot in the head, her jewels gone and neither her husband nor Velda was ever seen again."

I had to stop there. I didn't want to think on the next part anymore. I was hoping it would be enough for him, but when I looked up he was frowning with thought, digesting it a little at a time like he was diagnosing a disease, and I knew it wasn't finished yet.

He said, "They were abducted for the purpose of stealing those gems?"

"It was the only logical way they could do it. There were too many people. One scream would bring them running. They probably threatened the three of them, told them to move on out quietly where the theft could be done without interruption and allow the thieves to get away."

"Would Velda have gone along with them?"

"If they threatened the client that's the best way. It's better to give up insured gems than get killed. Even a rap on the head can kill if it isn't done right and, generally speaking, jewel thieves aren't killers unless they're pushed."

I felt a shudder go through my shoulders. "No. The body—showed why." I paused and he sat patiently, waiting. "Marta was a pudgy dame with thick fingers. She had crammed on three rings worth a hundred grand combined and they weren't about to come off normally. To get the rings they had severed the fingers."

Softly, he remarked, "I see."

"It was lousy."

"What do you think happened, Mike?"

I was going to hate to tell him, but it had been inside too long. I said, "Velda advised them to go along thinking it would be a heist without any physical complications. Probably when they started to take the rings off the hard way the woman started to scream and was shot. Then her husband and Velda tried to help her and that was it."

"Was what?"

I stared at the ceiling. Before it had been so plain, so simple. Totally believable because it had been so totally terrible. For all those years I had conditioned myself to think only one way because in my job you got to know which answers were right.

Now, suddenly, maybe they weren't right anymore.

Larry asked, "So they killed the man and Velda too and their bodies went out to sea and were never found?"

My tired tone was convincing. I said, "That's how the report read."

"So Pat took it all out on you."

"Looks that way."

"Uh-huh. You let her go on a job you should have handled yourself."

"It didn't seem that way at first."

"Perhaps, but you've been taking it out on yourself too. It just took that one thing to make you a bum."

"Hard words, friend."

"You realize what happened to Pat?"

I glanced at him briefly and nodded. "I found out."

"The hard way."

"So I didn't think he cared."

"You probably never would have known if that didn't happen."

"Kismet, buddy. Like your getting punched in the mouth."

"But there's a subtle difference now, Mikey boy, isn't there?"

"Like how?" I turned my head and watched him. He was the type who could hide his thoughts almost completely, even to a busted-up pro like me, but it didn't quite come off. I knew what he was getting to.

"Something new has been added, Mike."

"Oh?"

"You were a sick man not many hours ago."

"I'm hurting right now."

"You know what I'm talking about. You were a drunk just a little while back."

"So I kicked the habit."

"Why?"

"Seeing old friends helped."

He smiled at me, leaned forward and crossed his arms. "What did that guy tell you?"

"Nothing," I lied.

"I think I know. I think I know the only reason that would turn you from an acute alcoholic to a deadly sober man in a matter of minutes."

I had to be sure. I had to see what he knew. I said, "Tell me, Doc."

Larry stared at me a moment, smiled smugly and sat back, enjoying every second of the scene. When he thought my reaction would be just right he told me, "That guy mentioned the name of the killer."

So he couldn't see my face I turned my head. When I looked at him again he was still smiling, so I looked at the ceiling without answering and let him think what he pleased.

Larry said, "Now you're going out on your own, just like in the old days Pat used to tell me about."

"I haven't decided yet."

"Want some advice?"

"No."

"Nevertheless, you'd better spill it to Pat. He wants the same one."

"Pat can go drop."

"Maybe."

This time there was a peculiar intonation in his voice. I half turned and looked up at him. "Now what's bugging you?"

"Don't you think Pat knows you have something?"

"Like the man said, frankly, buddy, I don't give a damn."

"You won't tell me about it then?"

"You can believe it."

"Pat's going to lay charges on you."

"Good for him. When you clear out I'm going to have a lawyer ready who'll tear Pat apart. So maybe you'd better tell him."

"I will. But for your own sake, reconsider. It might be good for both of you."

Larry stood up and fingered the edge of his hat. A change came over his face and he grinned a little bit.

"Tell you something, Mike. I've heard so much about you it's like we're old friends. Just understand something. I'm really trying to help. Sometimes it's hard to be a doctor and a friend."

I held out my hand and grinned back. "Sure, I know. Forget that business about a paste in the mouth. You'd probably tear my head off."

He laughed and nodded, squeezed my hand and walked out. Before he reached the end of the corridor I was asleep again.

They make them patient in the government agencies. There was no telling how long he had been there. A small man, quiet, plain-looking—no indication of toughness unless you knew how to read it in his eyes. He just sat there as if he had all the time in the world and nothing to do except study me.

At least he had manners. He waited until I was completely awake before he reached for the little leather folder, opened it and said, "Art Rickerby, Federal Bureau of Investigation."

"No," I said sarcastically.

"You've been sleeping quite a while."

"What time is it?"

Without consulting his watch he said, "Five after four."

"It's pretty late."

Rickerby shrugged noncommittally without taking his eyes from my face. "Not for people like us," he told me. "It's never too late, is it?" He was smiling a small smile, but behind his glasses his eyes weren't smiling at all.

"Make your point, friend," I said.

He nodded thoughtfully, never losing his small smile. "Are you—let's say, capable of coherent discussion?"

"You've been reading my chart?"

"That's right. I spoke to your doctor friend too."

"Okay," I said, "forget the AA tag. I've had it, you know?"

"I know."

"Then what do we need the Feds in for? I've been out of action for how many years?"

"Seven."

"Long time, Art, long time, feller. I got no ticket, no rod. I haven't even crossed the state line in all that time. For seven years I cool myself off the way I want to and then all of a sudden I have a Fed on my neck." I squinted at him, trying to find the reason in his face. "Why?"

"Cole, Richie Cole."

"What about him?"

"Suppose you tell me, Mr. Hammer. He asked for you, you came and he spoke to you. I want to know what he said."

I reached way back and found a grin I thought I had forgotten how to make. "Everybody wants to know that, Rickeyback."

"Rickerby."

"So sorry." A laugh got in behind the grin. "Why all the curiosity?"

"Never mind why, just tell me what he said."

"Nuts, buddy."

He didn't react at all. He sat there with all the inbred patience of years of this sort of thing and simply looked at me tolerantly because I was in a bed in the funny ward and it might possibly be an excuse for anything I had to say or do.

Finally he said, "You *can* discuss this, can't you?"

I nodded. "But I won't."

"Why not?"

"I don't like anxious people. I've been kicked around, dragged into places I didn't especially want to go, kicked on my can by a cop who used to be a friend and suddenly faced with the prospects of formal charges because I object to the police version of the hard sell."

"Supposing I can offer you a certain amount of immunity?"

After a few moments I said, "This is beginning to get interesting."

Rickerby reached for words, feeling them out one at a time. "A long while ago you killed a woman, Mike. She shot a friend of yours and you said no matter who it was, no matter where, that killer would die. You shot her."

"Shut up, man," I said.

He was right. It was a very long time ago. But it could have been yesterday. I could see her face, the golden tan of her skin, the incredible whiteness of her hair and eyes that could taste and devour you with one glance. Yet, Charlotte was there still. But dead now.

"Hurt, Mike?"

There was no sense trying to fool him. I nodded abruptly. "I try not to think of it." Then I felt that funny sensation in my back and saw what he was getting at. His face was tight and the little lines around his eyes had deepened so that they stood out in relief, etched into his face.

I said, "You knew Cole?"

It was hard to tell what color his eyes were now. "He was one of us," he said.

I couldn't answer him. He had been waiting patiently a long time to say what he had to say and now it was going to come out. "We were close, Hammer. I trained him. I never had a son and he was as close as I was ever going to get to having one. Maybe now you know exactly why I brought up your past. It's mine who's dead now and it's me who has to find who did it. This should make sense to you. It should also tell you something else. Like you, I'll go to any extremes to catch the one who did it. I've made promises of my own, Mr. Hammer, and I'm sure you know what I'm talking about. Nothing is going to stop me and you are my starting point." He paused, took his glasses off, wiped them, put them back on and said, "You understand this?"

"I get the point."

"Are you sure?" And now his tone had changed. Very subtly, but changed nevertheless. "Because as I said, there are no extremes to which I won't go."

When he stopped I watched him and in the way he sat, the way he looked, the studied casualness became the poised kill-crouch of a cat, all cleverly disguised by clothes and the innocent aspect of rimless bifocals.

Now he was deadly. All too often people have the preconceived notion that a deadly person is a big one, wide in the shoulders with a face full of hard angles and thickset teeth and a jawline that would be a challenge too great for anyone to dare. They'd be wrong. Deadly people aren't all like that. Deadly people are determined people who will stop at nothing at all, and those who are practiced in the arts of the kill are the most deadly of all. Art Rickerby was one of those.

"That's not a very official attitude," I said.

"I'm just trying to impress you," he suggested.

I nodded. "Okay, kid, I'm impressed."

"Then what about Cole?"

"There's another angle."

"Not with me there isn't."

"Easy, Art, I'm not that impressed. I'm a big one too."

"No more, Hammer."

"Then you drop dead, too."

Like a large gray cat, he stood up, still pleasant, still deadly, and said, "I suppose we leave it here?"

"You pushed me, friend."

"It's a device you should be familiar with."

I was getting tired again, but I grinned a little at him. "Cops. Damn cops."

"You were one once."

After a while I said, "I never stopped being one."

"Then cooperate."

This time I turned my head and looked at him. "The facts are all bollixed up. I need one day and one other little thing you might be able to supply."

"Go ahead."

"Get me the hell out of here and get me that day."

"Then what?"

"Maybe I'll tell you something, maybe I won't. Just don't do me any outsized favors because if you don't bust me out of here I'll go out on my own. You can just make it easier. One way or another, I don't care. Take your pick."

Rickerby smiled. "I'll get you out," he said. "It won't be hard. And you can have your day."

"Thanks."

"Then come to me so I won't have to start looking for you."

"Sure, buddy," I said. "Leave your number at the desk."

He said something I didn't quite catch because I was falling asleep again, and when the welcome darkness came in I reached for it eagerly and wrapped it around me like a soft, dark suit of armor.

CHAPTER 4

He let me stay there three days before he moved. He let me have the endless bowls of soup and the bed rest and shot series before the tall thin man showed up with my clothes and a worried nurse whose orders had been countermanded somehow by an authority she neither understood nor could refuse.

When I was dressed he led me downstairs and outside to an unmarked black Ford and I got in without talking. He asked, "Where to?" and I told him anyplace midtown and in fifteen minutes he dropped me in front of the Taft. As I was getting out his hand closed on my arm and very quietly he said, "You have one day. No more."

I nodded. "Tell Rickerby thanks."

He handed me a card then, a simple business thing giving the address and phone of Peerage Brokers located on Broadway only two blocks off. "You tell him," he said, then pulled away from the curb into traffic.

For a few minutes I waited there, looking at the city in a strange sort of light I hadn't seen for too long. It was morning, and quiet because it was Sunday. Overhead, the sun forced its way through a haze that had rain behind it, making the day sulky, like a woman in a pout.

The first cabby in line glanced up once, ran his eyes up

and down me, then went back to his paper. Great picture, I thought. I sure must cut a figure. I grinned, even though nothing was funny, and shoved my hands in my jacket pockets. In the right-hand one somebody had stuck five tens, neatly folded and I said, "Thanks, Art Rickerby, old buddy," silently, and waved for the cab first in line to come over.

He didn't like it, but he came, asked me where to in a surly voice and when I let him simmer a little bit I told him Lex and Forty-ninth. When he dropped me there I let him change the ten, gave him two bits and waited some more to see if anyone had been behind me.

No one had. If Pat or anyone else had been notified I had been released, he wasn't bothering to stick with me. I gave it another five minutes then turned and walked north.

Old Dewey had held the same corner down for twenty years. During the war, servicemen got their paper free, which was about as much as he could do for the war effort, but there were those of us who never forgot and Old Dewey was a friend we saw often so that we were friends rather than customers. He was in his eighties now and he had to squint through his glasses to make out a face. But the faces of friends, their voices and their few minutes' conversation were things he treasured and looked forward to. Me? Hell, we were old friends from long ago, and back in the big days I never missed a night picking up my pink editions of the *News* and *Mirror* from Old Dewey, even when I had to go out of my way to do it. And there were times when I was in business that he made a good intermediary. He was always there, always dependable, never took a day off, never was on the take for a buck.

But he wasn't there now.

Duck-Duck Jones, who was an occasional swamper in the Clover Bar, sat inside the booth picking his teeth while he read the latest *Cavalier* magazine and it was only after I stood there a half minute that he looked up, scowled, then half-recognized me and said, "Oh, hello, Mike."

I said, "Hello, Duck-Duck. What are you doing here?"

He made a big shrug under his sweater and pulled his eyebrows up. "I help Old Dewey out alla time. Like when he eats. You know?"

"Where's he now?"

Once again, he went into an eloquent shrug. "So he don't show up yesterday. I take the key and open up for him. Today the same thing."

"Since when does Old Dewey miss a day?"

"Look, Mike, the guy's gettin' old. I take over maybe one day every week when he gets checked. Doc says he got something inside him, like. All this year he's been hurtin'."

"You keep the key?"

"Sure. We been friends a long time. He pays good. Better'n swabbing out the bar every night. This ain't so bad. Plenty of books with pictures. Even got a battery radio."

"He ever miss two days running?"

Duck-Duck made a face, thought a second and shook his head. "Like this is the first time. You know Old Dewey. He don't wanna miss nothin'. Nothin' at all."

"You check his flop?"

"Nah. You think I should? Like he could be sick or somethin'?"

"I'll do it myself."

"Sure, Mike. He lives right off Second by the diner, third place down in the basement. You got to—"

I nodded curtly. "I've been there."

"Look, Mike, if he don't feel good and wants me to stay on a bit I'll do it. I won't clip nothin'. You can tell him that."

"Okay, Duck."

I started to walk away and his voice caught me. "Hey, Mike."

"What?"

He was grinning through broken teeth, but his eyes were frankly puzzled. "You look funny, man. Like different from when I seen you last down at the Chink's. You off the hop?"

I grinned back at him. "Like for good," I said.

"Man, here we go again," he laughed.

"Like for sure," I told him.

Old Dewey owned the building. It wasn't much, but that and the newsstand were his insurance against the terrible thought of public support, a sure bulwark against the despised welfare plans of city and state. A second-rate beauty shop was on the ground floor and the top two were occupied by families who had businesses in the neighborhood. Old Dewey lived in humble quarters in the basement, needing only a single room in which to cook and sleep.

I tried his door, but the lock was secure. The only windows were those facing the street, the protective iron bars imbedded in the brickwork since the building had been erected. I knocked again, louder this time, and called out, but nobody answered.

Then again I had that funny feeling I had learned not to ignore, but it had been so long since I had felt it that it was almost new and once more I realized just how long it had been since I was in a dark place with a kill on my hands.

Back then it had been different. I had the gun. I was big. Now was—how many years later? There was no gun. I wasn't big anymore.

I was what was left over from being a damn drunken bum, and if there were anything left at all it was sheer reflex and nothing else.

So I called on the reflex and opened the door with the card the tall thin man gave me because it was an old lock with a wide gap in the doorframe. I shoved it back until it hit the door, standing there where anybody inside could target me easily, but knowing that it was safe because I had been close to death too many times not to recognize the immediate sound of silence it makes.

He was on the floor face down, arms outstretched, legs

spread, his head turned to one side so that he stared at one wall with the universal expression of the dead. He lay there in a pool of soup made from his own blood that had gouted forth from the great slash in his throat. The blood had long ago congealed and seeped into the cracks in the flooring, the coloring changed from scarlet to brown and already starting to smell.

Somebody had already searched the room. It hadn't taken long, but the job had been thorough. The signs of the expert were there, the one who had time and experience, who knew every possible hiding place and who had overlooked none. The search had gone around the room and come back to the body on the floor. The seams of the coat were carefully torn open, the pockets turned inside out, the shoes ripped apart.

But the door had been locked and this was not the sign of someone who had found what he wanted. Instead, it was the sign of he who hadn't and wanted time to think on it—or wait it out—or possibly study who else was looking for the same thing.

I said, "Don't worry, Dewey, I'll find him," and my voice was strangely hushed like it came from years ago. I wiped off the light switch, the knob, then closed the door and left it like I found it and felt my way to the back through the labyrinth of alleys that is New York over on that side and pretty soon I came out on the street again and it had started to rain.

His name was Nat Drutman. He owned the Hackard Building where I used to have my office and now, seven years later, he was just the same—only a little grayer and a little wiser around the eyes and when he glanced up at me from his desk it was as if he had seen me only yesterday.

"Hello, Mike."

"Nat."

"Good to see you."

"Thanks," I said.

This time his eyes stayed on me and he smiled, a gentle smile that had hope in it. "It has been a long time."

"Much too long."

"I know." He watched me expectantly.

I said, "You sell the junk from my office?"

"No."

"Store it?"

He shook his head, just once. "No."

"No games, kid," I said.

He made the Lower East Side gesture with his shoulders and let his smile stay pat. "It's still there, Mike."

"Not after seven years, kid," I told him.

"That's so long?"

"For somebody who wants their loot it is."

"So who needs loot?"

"Nat—"

"Yes, Mike?"

His smile was hard to understand.

"No games."

"You still got a key?" he asked.

"No I left to stay. No key. No nothing anymore."

He held out his hand, offering me a shiny piece of brass. I took it automatically and looked at the number stamped into it, a fat 808. "I had it made special," he said.

As best I could, I tried to be nasty. "Come off it, Nat."

He wouldn't accept the act. "Don't thank me. I knew you'd be back."

I said, "Shit."

There was a hurt look on his face. It barely touched his eyes and the corners of his mouth, but I knew I had hurt him.

"Seven years, Nat. That's a lot of rent."

He wouldn't argue. I got that shrug again and the funny look that went with it. "So for you I dropped the rent to a dollar a year while you were gone."

I looked at the key, feeling my shoulders tighten. "Nat—"

"Please—don't talk. Just take. Remember when you gave? Remember Bernie and those men? Remember—"

"Okay, Nat."

The sudden tension left his face and he smiled again. I said, "Thanks, kid. You'll never know."

A small laugh left his lips and he said, "Oh I'll know, all right. That'll be seven dollars. Seven years, seven dollars."

I took out another ten and laid it on his desk. With complete seriousness he gave me back three ones, a receipt, then said, "You got a phone too, Mike. Same number. No 'thank yous,' Mike. Augie Strickland came in with the six hundred he owed you and left it with me so I paid the phone bill from it. You still got maybe a couple bucks coming back if we figure close."

"Save it for service charges," I said.

"Good to see you, Mike."

"Good to see you, Nat."

"You look pretty bad. Is everything going to be like before, Mike?"

"It can never be like before. Let's hope it's better."

"Sure, Mike."

"And thanks anyway, kid."

"My pleasure, Mike."

I looked at the key, folded it in my fist and started out. When I reached the door Nat said, "Mike—"

I turned around.

"Velda . . . ?"

He watched my eyes closely.

"That's why you're back?"

"Why?"

"I hear many stories, Mike. Twice I even saw you. Things I know that nobody else knows. I know why you left. I know why you came back. I even waited because I knew someday you'd come. So you're back. You don't look like you did except for your eyes. They never change. Now you're all beat up and skinny and far behind. Except for your eyes, and that's the worst part."

"Is it?"

He nodded. "For somebody," he said.

I put the key in the lock and turned the knob. It was like coming back to the place where you had been born, remembering, yet without a full recollection of all the details. It was a drawing, wanting power that made me swing the door open because I wanted to see how it used to be and how it might have been.

Her desk was there in the anteroom, the typewriter still covered, letters from years ago stacked in a neat pile waiting to be answered, the last note she had left for me still there beside the phone some itinerant spider had draped in a nightgown of cobwebs.

The wastebasket was where I had kicked it, dented almost double from my foot; the two captain's chairs and antique bench we used for clients were still overturned against the wall where I had thrown them. The door to my office swung open, tendrils of webbing seeming to tie it to the frame. Behind it I could see my desk and chair outlined in the gray shaft of light that was all that was left of the day.

I walked in, waving the cobwebs apart, and sat down in the chair. There was dust, and silence, and I was back to seven years ago, all of a sudden. Outside the window was another New York—not the one I had left, because the old one had been torn down and rebuilt since I had looked out that window last. But below on the street the sounds hadn't changed a bit, nor had the people. Death and destruction were still there, the grand overseers of life toward the great abyss, some slowly, some quickly, but always along the same road.

For a few minutes I just sat there swinging in the chair, recalling the feel and the sound of it. I made a casual inspection of the desk drawers, not remembering what was there, yet enjoying a sense of familiarity with old things. It was an old desk, almost antique, a relic from some solid, conservative corporation that supplied its executives with the best.

When you pulled the top drawer all the way out there was a niche built into the massive framework, and when I felt in the shallow recess the other relic was still there.

Calibre .45, Colt Automatic, U.S. Army model, vintage of 1914. Inside the plastic wrapper it was still oiled, and when I checked the action it was like a thing alive, a deadly thing that had but a single fundamental purpose.

I put it back where it was beside the box of shells, inserted the drawer and slid it shut. The day of the guns was back there seven years ago. Not now.

Now I was one of the nothing people. One mistake and Pat had me, and where I was going, one mistake and *they* would have me.

Pat. The slob really took off after me. I wondered if Larry had been right when he said Pat had been in love with Velda too?

I nodded absently, because he had changed. And there was more to it, besides. In seven years Pat should have moved up the ladder. By now he should have been an Inspector. Maybe whatever it was he had crawling around in his guts got out of hand and he never made the big try for promotion, or, if he did, he loused up.

The hell with him, I thought. Now he was going wide open to nail a killer and a big one. Whoever killed Richie Cole had killed Senator Knapp in all probability, and in all probability, too, had killed Old Dewey. Well, I was one up on Pat. He'd have another kill in his lap, all right, but only I could connect Dewey and the others.

Which put me in the middle all around.

So okay, Hammer, I said. You've been a patsy before. See what you'll do with this one and do it right. Someplace she's alive. Alive! But for how long? And where? There are killers loose and she must be on the list.

Absently, I reached for the phone, grinned when I heard the dial tone, then fingered the card the thin man gave me from my pocket and called Peerage Brokers.

He was there waiting and when I asked, "Rickerby?" a switch clicked.

Art answered, "You still have a little more time."

"I don't need time. I need now. I think we should talk."

"Where are you?"

"My own office through courtesy of a friend. The Hackard Building."

"Stay there. I'll be up in ten minutes."

"Sure. Bring me a sandwich."

"A drink too?"

"None of that. Maybe a couple of Blue Ribbons, but nothing else."

Without answering, he hung up. I glanced at my wrist, but there was no watch there anymore. Somehow, I vaguely remembered hocking it somewhere and called myself a nut because it was a good Rollex and I probably drank up the loot in half a day. Or got rolled for it.

Damn!

From the window I could see the clock on the Paramount Building and it was twenty past six. The street was slick from the drizzle that had finally started to fall and the crosstown traffic was like a giant worm trying to eat into the belly of the city. I opened the window and got supper smells in ten languages from the restaurants below and for the first time in a long time it smelled good. Then I switched on the desk lamp and sat back again.

Rickerby came in, put a wrapped sandwich and two cans of Blue Ribbon in front of me and sat down with a weary smile. It was a very peculiar smile, not of friendliness, but of anticipation. It was one you didn't smile back at, but rather waited out.

And I made him wait until I had finished the sandwich and a can of beer, then I said, "Thanks for everything."

Once again, he smiled. "Was it worth it?"

His eyes had that flat calm that was nearly impenetrable. I said, "Possibly. I don't know. Not yet."

"Suppose we discuss it."

I smiled some too. The way his face changed I wondered what I looked like. "It's all right with me, Rickety."

"Rickerby."

"Sorry," I said. "But let's do it question-and-answer style. Only I want to go first."

"You're not exactly in a position to dictate terms."

"I think I am. I've been put upon. You know?"

He shrugged, and looked at me again, still patient. "It really doesn't matter. Ask me what you want to."

"Are you officially on this case?"

Rickerby didn't take too long putting it in its proper category. It would be easy enough to plot out if you knew how, so he simply made a vague motion with his shoulders. "No. Richie's death is at this moment a local police matter."

"Do they know who he was?"

"By now, I assume so."

"And your department won't press the matter?"

He smiled, nothing more.

I said, "Suppose I put it this way—if his death resulted in the line of duty he was pursuing—because of the case he was on, then your department would be interested."

Rickerby looked at me, his silence acknowledging my statement.

"However," I continued, "if he was the victum of circumstances that could hit anybody, it would remain a local police matter and his other identity would remain concealed from everyone possible. True?"

"You seem familiar enough with the machinations of our department, so draw your own conclusions," Rickerby told me.

"I will. I'd say that presently it's up in the air. You're on detached duty because of a personal interest in this thing. You couldn't be ordered off it, otherwise you'd resign and pursue it yourself."

"You know, Mike, for someone who was an alcoholic such a short time ago, your mind is awfully lucid." He took his glasses off and wiped them carefully before putting them back on. "I'm beginning to be very interested in this aspect of your personality."

"Let me clue you, buddy. It was shock. I was brought back to my own house fast, and suddenly meeting death in a sober condition really rocked me."

"I'm not so sure of that," he said. "Nevertheless, get on with your questions."

"What was Richie Cole's job?"

After a moment's pause he said, "Don't be silly. I certainly don't know. If I did I wouldn't reveal it."

"Okay, what was his cover?"

All he did was shake his head and smile.

I said, "You told me you'd do anything to get the one who killed him."

This time a full minute passed before he glanced down at his hands, then back to me again. In that time he had done some rapid mental calculations. "I—don't see how it could matter now," he said. When he paused a sadness creased his mouth momentarily, then he went on. "Richie worked as a seaman."

"Union man?"

"That's right. He held a full card."

CHAPTER 5

The elevator operator in the Trib Building looked at me kind of funny like when I told him I wanted to find Hy. But maybe Hy had all kinds of hooples looking for him at odd hours. At one time the guy would never have asked questions, but now was now. The old Mike wasn't quite there any more.

In gold, the letters said, HY GARDNER. I knocked, opened the door and there he was, staring until recognition came, and with a subtle restraint he said, "Mike—" It was almost a question.

"A long time, Hy."

But always the nice guy, this one. Never picking, never choosing. He said, "Been too long. I've been wondering."

"So have a lot of people."

"But not for the same reasons."

We shook hands, a couple of old friends saying hello from a long while back; we had both been big, but while he had gone ahead and I had faded, yet still friends and good ones.

He tried to cover the grand hiatus of so many years with a cigar stuck in the middle of a smile and made it all the way, without words telling me that nothing had really

52

changed at all since the first time we had played bullets in a bar and he had made a column out of it the next day.

Hell, you've read his stuff. You know us.

I sat down, waved the crazy blonde bouffant he used as a secretary now out of the room and leaned back enjoying myself. After seven years it was a long time to enjoy anything. Friends.

I still had them.

"You look lousy," Hy said.

"So I've been told."

"True what I hear about you and Pat?"

"Word gets around fast."

"You know this business, Mike."

"Sure, so don't bother being kind."

"You're a nut," he laughed.

"Aren't we all. One kind or another."

"Sure, but you're on top. You know the word that's out right now?"

"I can imagine."

"The hell you can. You don't even know. What comes in this office you couldn't imagine. When they picked you up I heard about it. When you were in Pat's house I knew where you were. If you really want to know, whenever you were in the drunk tank, unidentified, I knew about it."

"Cripes, why didn't you get me out?"

"Mike," he laughed around the stogie, "I got problems of my own. When you can't solve yours, who can solve anything? Besides, I thought it would be a good experience for you."

"Thanks."

"No bother." He shifted the cigar from one side to the other. "But I was worried."

"Well, that's nice anyway," I said.

"Now it's worse."

Hy took the cigar away, studied me intently, stuffed the smoke out in a tray and pulled his eyes up to mine.

"Mike—"

"Say it, Hy."

He was honest. He pulled no punches. It was like time

had never been at all and we were squaring away for the first time. "You're poison, Mike. The word's out."

"To you?"

"No." He shook his head. "They don't touch the Fifth Estate, you know that. They tried it with Joe Ungermach and Victor Reisel and look what happened to them. So don't worry about me."

"You worried about me?"

Hy grunted, lit another cigar and grinned at me. He had his glasses up on his head and you'd never think he could be anything but an innocuous slob, but then you'd be wrong. When he had it lit, he said, "I gave up worrying about you a long time ago. Now what did you want from me? It has to be big after seven years."

"Senator Knapp," I said.

Sure, he was thinking, *after seven years who the hell would think you'd come back with a little one? Mike Hammer chasing ambulances? Mike Hammer suddenly a reformer or coming up with a civic problem? Hell, anybody would have guessed. The Mike doesn't come back without a big one going. This a kill, Mike? What's the scoop? Story there, isn't there? You have a killer lined up just like in the old days and don't lie to me because I've seen those tiger eyes before. If they were blue or brown like anybody else's maybe I couldn't tell, but you got tiger eyes, friend, and they glint. So tell me. Tell me hard. Tell me now.*

He didn't have to say it. Every word was there in his face, like when he had read it out to me before. I didn't have to hear it now. Just looking at him was enough.

I said, "Senator Knapp. He died when I was—away."

Quietly, Hy reminded me, "He didn't die. He was killed."

"Okay. The libraries were closed and besides, I forgot my card."

"He's been dead three years."

"More."

"First why?"

"Because."

"You come on strong, man."

"You know another way?"

"Not for you."

"So how about the Senator?"

"Are we square?" he asked me. "It can be my story?"

"All yours, Hy. I don't make a buck telling columns."

"Got a few minutes?"

"All right," I said.

He didn't even have to consult the files. All he had to do was light that damn cigar again and sit back in his chair, then he sucked his mouth full of smoke and said, "Leo Knapp was another McCarthy. He was a Commie-hunter but he had more prestige and more power. He was on the right committee and, to top it off, he was this country's missile man."

"That's what they called him, the *Missile Man*. Mr. America. He pulled hard against the crap we put up with like the Cape Canaveral strikes when the entire program was held up by stupid jerks who went all that way for unionism and—hell, read *True* or the factual accounts and see what happened. The Reds are running us blind. Anyway, Knapp was the missile pusher."

"Big," I said.

Hy nodded. "Then some louse shoots him. A simple burglary and he gets killed in the process."

"You sure?"

Hy looked at me, the cigar hard in his teeth. "You know me, Mike, I'm a reporter. I'm a Commie-hater. You think I didn't take this one right into the ground?"

"I can imagine what you did."

"Now fill me in."

"Can you keep your mouth shut?"

He took the cigar away and frowned, like I had hurt him. "Mike—"

"Look," I said, "I know, I know. But I may feed you a hot one and I have to be sure. Until it's ended, it can't come out. There's something here too big to mess with and I won't even take a little chance on it."

"So tell me. I know what you're angling for. Your old

contacts are gone or poisoned and you want me to shill for you."

"Natch."

"So I'll shill. Hell, we've done it before. It won't be like it's a new experience."

"And keep Marilyn out of it. To her you're a new husband and a father and she doesn't want you going down bullet alley anymore."

"Aw, shut up and tell me what's on your mind."

I did.

I sat back and told it all out and let somebody else help carry the big lid. I gave it to him in detail from seven years ago and left out nothing. I watched his face go through all the changes, watched him let the cigar burn itself out against the lip of the ashtray, watched him come alive with the crazy possibilities that were inherent in this one impossibility and when I finished I watched him sit back, light another cigar and regain his usual composure.

When he had it back again he said, "What do you want from me?"

"I don't know. It could be anything."

Like always, Hy nodded. "Okay, Mike. When it's ready to blow let me light the fuse. Hell, maybe we can do an interview with the about-to-be-deceased on the TV show ahead of time."

"No jokes, kid."

"Ah, cheer up. Things could be worse."

"I know," I quoted, " 'So I cheered up and sure enough things got worse.' "

Hy grinned and knocked the ash off the stogie. "Right now—anything you need?"

"Senator Knapp—"

"Right now his widow is at her summer place upstate in Phoenicia. That's where the Senator was shot."

"You'd think she'd move out."

Hy shrugged gently. "That's foolishness, in a way. It was the Senator's favorite home and she keeps it up. The rest of the year she stays at the residence in Washington.

In fact, Laura is still one of the capital's favorite hostesses. Quite a doll."

"Oh?"

He nodded sagely, the cigar at an authoritative tilt. "The Senator was all man and what he picked was all woman. They were a great combination. It'll be a long time before you see one like that again."

"Tough."

"That's the way it goes. Look, if you want the details, I'll have a package run out from the morgue."

"I'd appreciate that."

Two minutes after he made his call a boy came through with a thick Manila envelope and laid it on the desk. Hy hefted it, handed it over and said: "This'll give you all the background on the murder. It made quite a story."

"Later there will be more."

"Sure," he agreed, "I know how you work."

I got up and put on my hat. "Thanks."

"No trouble, Mike." He leaned back in his chair and pulled his glasses down. "Be careful, Mike. You look lousy."

"Don't worry."

"Just the same, don't stick your neck out. Things can change in a few years. You're not like you were. A lot of people would like to catch up with you right now."

I grinned back at him. "I think most already have."

You drive up the New York Thruway, get off at Kingston and take the mountain route through some of the most beautiful country in the world. At Phoenicia you turn off to the north for five or six miles until you come to The Willows and there is the chalet nestling in the upcurve of the mountain, tended by blue spruces forty feet high and nursed by a living stream that dances its way in front of it.

It was huge and white and very senatorial, yet there was a lived-in look that took away any pretentiousness. It was a money house and it should have been because the Senator had been a money man. He had made it himself and had spent it the way he liked and this had been a pet project.

I went up through the gentle curve of the drive and shut off the motor in front of the house. When I touched the bell I could hear it chime inside, and after a minute of standing there, I touched it again. Still no one answered.

Just to be sure, I came down off the open porch, skirted the house on a flagstone walk that led to the rear and followed the S turns through the shrubbery arrangement that effectively blocked off all view of the back until you were almost on top of it.

There was a pool on one side and a tennis court on the other. Nestling between them was a green-roofed cottage with outside shower stalls that was obviously a dressing house.

At first I thought it was deserted here too, then very faintly I heard the distance-muffled sound of music. A hedgerow screened the southeast corner of the pool and in the corner of it the multicolor top of a table umbrella showed through the interlocking branches.

I stood there a few seconds, just looking down at her. Her hands were cradled behind her head, her eyes were closed and she was stretched out to the sun in taut repose. The top of the two-piece bathing suit was filled to overflowing with a matured ripeness that was breathtaking; the bottom half turned down well below her dimpled navel in a bikini effect, exposing the startling whiteness of untanned flesh against that which had been sun-kissed. Her breathing shallowed her stomach, then swelled it gently, and she turned slightly, stretching, pointing her toes so that a sinuous ripple of muscles played along her thighs.

I said, "Hello."

Her eyes came open, focused sleepily and she smiled at me. "Oh." Her smile broadened and it was like throwing a handful of beauty in her face. "Oh, hello."

Without being asked I handed her the terry-cloth robe that was thrown across the tabletop. She took it, smiled again and threw it around her shoulders. "Thank you."

"Isn't it a little cold for that sort of thing?"

"Not in the sun." She waved to the deck chair beside her. "Please?" When I sat down she rearranged her lounge into a chair and settled back in it. "Now, Mr.—"

"Hammer. Michael Hammer." I tried on a smile for her too. "And you are Laura Knapp?"

"Yes. Do I know you from somewhere, Mr. Hammer?"

"We've never met."

"But there's something familiar about you."

"I used to get in the papers a lot."

"Oh?" It was a full-sized question.

"I was a private investigator at one time."

She frowned, studying me, her teeth white against the lushness of her lip as she nibbled at it. "There was an affair with a Washington agency at one time—"

I nodded.

"I remember it well. My husband was on a committee that was affected by it." She paused. "So you're Mike Hammer." Her frown deepened.

"You expected something more?"

Her smile was mischievous. "I don't quite know. Perhaps."

"I've been sick," I said, grinning.

"Yes," she told me, "I can believe that. Now, the question is, what are you doing here? Is this part of your work?"

There was no sense lying to her. I said, "No, but there's a possibility you can help me."

"How?"

"Do you mind going over the details of your husband's murder, or is it too touchy a subject?"

This time her smile took on a wry note. "You're very blunt, Mr. Hammer. However, it's something in the past and I'm not afraid to discuss it. You could have examined the records of the incident if you wanted to. Wouldn't that have been easier?"

I let my eyes travel over her and let out a laugh. "I'm glad I came now."

Laura Knapp laughed back. "Well, thank you."

"But in case you're wondering, I did go over the clips on the case."

"And that wasn't enough?"

I shrugged. "I don't know. I'd rather hear it firsthand."

"May I ask why?"

"Sure," I said. "Something has come up that might tie in your husband's killer with another murder."

Laura shook her head slowly. "I don't understand—"

"It's a wild supposition, that's all, a probability I'm trying to chase down. Another man was killed with the same gun that shot your husband. Details that seemed unimportant then might have some bearing now."

"I see." She came away from the chair, leaning toward me with her hands hugging her knees, a new light of interest in her eyes. "But why aren't the police here instead of you?"

"They will be. Right now it's a matter of jurisdiction. Very shortly you'll be seeing a New York City officer, probably accompanied by the locals, who will go over the same ground. I don't have any legal paperwork to go through so I got here first."

Once again she started a slow smile and let it play around her mouth a moment before she spoke. "And if I don't talk—will you belt me one?"

"Hell," I said, "I never hit dames."

Her eyebrows went up in mock surprise.

"I always kick 'em."

The laugh she let out was pleasant and throaty and it was easy to see why she was still queen of the crazy social whirl at the capital. Age never seemed to have touched her, though she was in the loveliest early forties. Her hair shimmered with easy blond highlights, a perfect shade to go with the velvety sheen of her skin.

"I'll talk," she laughed, "but do I get a reward if I do?"

"Sure, I won't kick you."

"Sounds enticing. What do you want to know?"

"Tell me what happened."

She reflected a moment. It was evident that the details were there, stark as ever in her mind, though the thought didn't bring the pain back any longer. She finally said, "It was a little after two in the morning. I heard Leo get up but didn't pay any attention to it since he often went down for nighttime snacks. The next thing I heard was his voice shouting at someone, then a single shot. I got up, ran downstairs and there he was on the floor, dying."

"Did he say anything?"

"No—he called out my name twice, then he died." She looked down at her feet, then glanced up. "I called the police. Not immediately. I was—stunned."

"It happens."

She chewed at her lip again. "The police were inclined to—well, they were annoyed. They figured the person had time to get away." Her eyes clouded, then drifted back in time. "But it couldn't have been more than a few minutes. No more. In fact, there could have been no time at all before I called. It's just that I don't remember those first few moments."

"Forget it anyway," I said. "That part doesn't count any more."

Laura paused, then nodded in agreement. "You're right, of course. Well, then the police came, but there was nothing they could do. Whoever it was had gone through the French windows in the den, then had run across the yard, gone through the gate and driven away. There were no tire tracks and the footprints he left were of no consequence."

"What about the house?"

She wrinkled her forehead as she looked over at me. "The safe was open and empty. The police believe Leo either surprised the burglar after he opened the safe or the burglar made him open the safe and when Leo went for him, killed him. There were no marks on the safe at all. It had been opened by using the combination."

"How many people knew the combination?"

"Just Leo, as far as I know."

I said, "The papers stated that nothing of importance was in the safe."

"That's right. There couldn't have been over a few

hundred dollars in cash, a couple of account books, Leo's insurance policies, some legal papers and some jewelry of mine. The books and legal papers were on the floor intact so—"

"What jewelry?" I interrupted.

"It was junk."

"The papers quoted you as saying about a thousand dollars' worth."

She didn't hesitate and there was no evasion in her manner. "That's right, a thousand dollars' worth of paste. They were replicas of the genuine pieces I keep in a vault. That value is almost a hundred thousand dollars."

"A false premise is as good a reason for robbery as any."

Her eyes said she didn't agree with me. "Nobody knew I kept that paste jewelry in there."

"Two people did."

"Oh?"

I said, "Your husband and his killer."

The implication of it finally came to her. "He wouldn't have mentioned it to anyone. No, you're wrong there. It wasn't that important to him at all."

"Then why put it in the safe?"

"It's a natural place for it. Besides, as you mentioned, it could be a strong come-on to one who didn't know any better."

"Why didn't you have the combination?"

"I didn't need it. It was the only safe in the house, in Leo's private study—and, concerning his affairs, I stayed out completely."

"Servants?"

"At that time we had two. Both were very old and both have since died. I don't think they ever suspected that there were two sets of jewels anyway."

"Were they trustworthy?"

"They had been with Leo all his life. Yes, they were trustworthy."

I leaned back in the chair, reaching hard for any possibility now. "Could anything else have been in that safe? Something you didn't know about?"

"Certainly."

I edged forward now, waiting.

"Leo *could* have kept anything there, but I doubt that he did. I believe you're thinking of what could be termed state secrets?"

"It's happened before. The Senator was a man pretty high in the machinery of government."

"And a smart one," she countered. "His papers that had governmental importance were all intact in his safe-deposit box and were recovered immediately after his death by the FBI, according to a memo he left with his office." She waited a moment then, watching me try to fasten on some obscure piece of information. Then she asked, "May I know what you're trying to get at?"

This time there was no answer. Very simply the whole thing broke down to a not unusual coincidence. One gun had been used for two kills. It happens often enough. These kills had been years apart, and from all the facts, totally unrelated.

I said, "It was a try, that's all. Nothing seems to match."

Quietly, she stated, "I'm sorry."

"Couldn't be helped." I stood up, not quite wanting to terminate our discussion. "It might have been the jewels, but a real pro would have made sure of what he was going after, and this isn't exactly the kind of place an amateur would hit."

Laura held out her hand and I took it, pulling her to her feet. It was like an unwinding, like a large fireside cat coming erect, yet so naturally that you were never aware of any artifice, but only the similarity. "Are you sure there's nothing further . . . ?"

"Maybe one thing," I said. "Can I see the den?"

She nodded, reaching out to touch my arm. "Whatever you want."

While she changed she left me alone in the room. It was a man's place, where only a man could be comfortable, a place designed and used by a man used to living. The desk was an oversized piece of deep-colored wood, almost antique in style, offset by dark leather chairs and original oil seascapes. The walnut paneling was hand carved, years old and well polished, matching the worn oriental rug that must have come over on a Yankee clipper ship.

The wall safe was a small circular affair that nestled behind a two-by-three-foot picture, the single modern touch in the room. Laura had opened the desk drawer, extracted a card containing the combination and handed it to me. Alone, I dialed the seven numbers and swung the safe out. It was empty.

That I had expected. What I hadn't expected was the safe itself. It was a Grissom 914A and was not the type you installed to keep junk jewelry or inconsequential papers in. This safe was more than a fireproof receptacle and simple safeguard for trivia. This job had been designed to be burglar-proof and had a built-in safety factor on the third number that would have been hooked into the local police PBX at the very least. I closed it, dialed it once again using the secondary number, opened it and waited.

Before Laura came down the cops were there, two excited young fellows in a battered Ford who came to the door with Police Specials out and ready, holding them at my gut when I let them in and looking able to use them.

The taller of the pair went around me while the other looked at me carefully and said, "Who're you?"

"I'm the one who tuned you in."

"Don't get smart."

"I was testing the wall safe out."

His grin had a wicked edge to it. "You don't test it like that, buddy."

"Sorry. I should have called first."

He went to answer, but his partner called in from the front room and he waved me ahead with the nose of the .38. Laura and the cop were there, both looking puzzled.

Laura had changed into a belted black dress that accented the sweeping curves of her body and when she stepped across the room toward me it was with the lithe grace of an athlete. "Mike—do you know what—"

"Your safe had an alarm number built into it. I checked it to see if it worked. Apparently it did."

"That right, Mrs. Knapp?" the tall cop asked.

"Well, yes. I let Mr. Hammer inspect the safe. I didn't realize it had an alarm on it."

"It's the only house around here that has that system, Mrs. Knapp. It's more or less on a commercial setup."

Beside me the cop holstered his gun with a shrug. "That's that," he said. "It was a good try."

The other one nodded, adjusted his cap and looked across at me. "We'd appreciate your calling first if it happens again."

"Sure thing. Mind a question?"

"Nope."

"Were you on the force when the Senator was killed?"

"We both were."

"Did the alarm go off then?"

The cop gave me a long, deliberate look, his face wary, then, "No, it didn't."

"Then if the killer opened the safe he knew the right combination."

"Or else," the cop reminded me, "he forced the Senator to open it, and knowing there was nothing of real value in there, and not willing to jeopardize his own or his wife's life by sudden interference, the Senator didn't use the alarm number."

"But he was killed anyway," I reminded him.

"If you had known the Senator you could see why."

"Okay, why?" I asked him.

Softly, the cop said: "If he was under a gun he'd stay there, but given one chance to jump the guy and he'd have jumped. Apparently he thought he saw the chance and went for the guy after the safe was open and just wasn't fast enough."

"Or else surprised the guy when the safe was already opened."

"That's the way it still reads." He smiled indulgently.

"We had those angles figured out too, you know. Now do you mind telling me where you fit in the picture?"

"Obscurely. A friend of mine was killed by a bullet from the same gun."

The two cops exchanged glances. The one beside me said, "We didn't hear about that part yet."

"Then you will shortly. You'll be speaking to a Captain Chambers from New York sometime soon."

"That doesn't explain you."

I shrugged. "The guy was a friend."

"Do you represent a legal investigation agency?"

"No longer," I told him. "There was a time when I did."

"Then maybe you ought to leave the investigation up to authorized personnel."

His meaning was obvious. If I hadn't been cleared by Laura Knapp and tentatively accepted as her friend, we'd be doing our talking in the local precinct house. It was a large Keep Off sign he was pointing out and he wasn't kidding about it. I made a motion with my hand to let him know I got the message, watched them tip their caps to Laura and walk out.

When they had pulled away Laura said, "Now what was *that* all about?" She stood balanced on one foot, her hands on her hips in an easy, yet provocative manner, frowning slightly as she tried to sift through the situation.

I said, "Didn't you know there was an alarm system built into that box?"

She thought for a moment, then threw a glance toward the wall. "Yes, now that you mention it, but that safe hasn't been opened since—then, and I simply remember the police discussing an alarm system. I didn't know how it worked at all."

"Did your husband always keep that combination card in his desk?"

"No, the lawyer found it in his effects. I kept it in the desk just in case I ever wanted to use the safe again. However, that never happened." She paused, took a step toward me and laid a hand on my arm. "Is there some significance to all this?"

I shook my head. "I don't know. It was a thought and not a very new one. Like I told you, this was only a wild supposition at best. All I can say is that it might have established an M.O."

"What?"

"A technique of operation," I explained. "Your husband's killer really could have gone after those jewels. The other man he killed was operating—well, was a small-time jewel smuggler. There's a common point here."

For a moment I was far away in thought. I was back in the hospital with a dying man, remembering the reason why I wanted to find that link so badly. I could feel claws pulling at my insides and a fierce tension ready to burst apart like an overwound spring.

It was the steady insistence of her voice that dragged me back to the present, her "Mike—Mike—please, Mike."

When I looked down I saw my fingers biting into her forearm and the quiet pain in her eyes. I let her go and sucked air deep into my lungs. "Sorry," I said.

She rubbed her arm and smiled gently. "That's all right. You left me there for a minute, didn't you?"

I nodded.

"Can I help?"

"No. I don't think there's anything more here for me."

Once again, her hand touched me. "I don't like finalities like that, Mike."

It was my turn to grin my thanks. "I'm not all that sick. But I appreciate the thought."

"You're lonely, Mike. That's a sickness."

"Is it?"

"I've had it so long I can recognize it in others."

"You loved him very much, didn't you?"

Her eyes changed momentarily, seeming to shine a little brighter, then she replied, "As much as you loved her, Mike, whoever she was." Her fingers tightened slightly. "It's a big hurt. I eased mine by all the social activity I could crowd in a day."

"I used a bottle. It was a hell of a seven years."

"And now it's over. I can still see the signs, but I can tell it's over."

"It's over. A few days ago I was a drunken bum. I'm still a bum but at least I'm sober." I reached for my hat, feeling her hand fall away from my arm. She walked me to the door and held it open. When I stuck out my hand she took it, her fingers firm and cool inside mine. "Thanks for letting me take up your time, Mrs. Knapp."

"Please—make it Laura."

"Sure."

"And can you return the favor?"

"My pleasure."

"I told you I didn't like finalities. Will you come back one day?"

"I'm nothing to want back Laura."

"Maybe not to some. You're big. You have a strange face. You're very hard to define. Still, I hope you'll come back, if only to tell me how you're making out."

I pulled her toward me gently. She didn't resist. Her head tilted up, she watched me, she kissed me as I kissed her, easily and warm in a manner that said hello rather than goodbye, and that one touch awakened things I thought had died long ago.

She stood there watching me as I drove away. She was still there when I turned out of sight at the roadway.

CHAPTER 6

The quiet voice at Peerage Brokers told me I would be able to meet with Mr. Rickerby in twenty minutes at the Automat on Sixth and Forty-fifth. When I walked in he was off to the side, coffee in front of him, a patient little gray man who seemingly had all the time in the world.

I put down my own coffee, sat opposite him and said, "You have wild office hours."

He smiled meaninglessly, a studied, yet unconscious gesture that was for anyone watching. But there was no patience in his eyes. They seemed to live by themselves, being held in check by some obscure force. The late edition of the *News* was folded back to the center spread where a small photo gave an angular view of Old Dewey dead on the floor. The cops had blamed it on terrorists in the neighborhood.

Rickerby waited me out until I said, "I saw Laura Knapp today," then he nodded.

"We covered that angle pretty thoroughly."

"Did you know about the safe? It had an alarm system."

Once again, he nodded. "For your information, I'll tell you this. No connection has been made by any department between Senator Knapp's death and that of Richie. If you're assuming any state papers were in that safe you're wrong. Knapp had duplicate listings of every paper he had in his possession and we recovered everything."

"There were those paste jewels," I said.

"I know. I doubt if they establish anything, even in view of Richie's cover. It seems pretty definite that the gun was simply used in different jobs. As a matter of fact, Los Angeles has since come up with another murder in which the same gun was used. This was a year ago and the victim was a used-car dealer."

"So it wasn't a great idea."

"Nor original." He put down his coffee and stared at me across the table. "Nor am I interested in others besides Richie." He paused, let a few seconds pass, then added, "Have you decided to tell me what Richie really told you?"

"No."

"At least I won't have to call you a liar again."

"Knock it off."

Rickerby's little smile faded slowly and he shrugged. "Make your point then."

"Cole. I want to know about him."

"I told you once—"

"Okay, so it's secret. But now he's dead. You want a killer, I want a killer and if we don't get together someplace nobody gets nothing. You know?"

His fingers tightened on the cup, the nails showing the strain. He let a full minute pass before he came to a decision. He said, "Can you imagine how many persons are looking for this—killer?"

"I've been in the business too, friend."

"All right. I'll tell you this. I know nothing of Richie's last mission and I doubt if I'll find out. But this much I do know—he wasn't supposed to be back here at all. He disobeyed orders and would have been on the carpet had he not been killed."

I said, "Cole wasn't a novice."

And for the first time Rickerby lost his composure. His eyes looked puzzled, bewildered at this sudden failure of something he had built himself. "That's the strange part about it."

"Oh?"

"Richie was forty-five years old. He had been with one department or another since '41 and his record was perfect. He was a book man through and through and wouldn't bust a reg for any reason. He could adapt if the situation necessitated it, but it would conform to certain regulations." He stopped, looked across his cup at me and shook his head slowly. "I—just can't figure it."

"Something put him here."

This time his eyes went back to their bland expression. He had allowed himself those few moments and that was all. Now he was on the job again, the essence of many years of self-discipline, nearly emotionless to the casual observer. "I know," he said.

And he waited and watched for me to give him the one word that might send him out on a kill chase. I used my own coffee cup to cover what I thought, ran through the possibilities until I knew what I wanted and leaned back in my chair. "I need more time," I told him.

"Time isn't too important to me. Richie's dead. Time would be important only if it meant keeping him alive."

"It's important to me."

"How long do you need before telling me?"

"Telling what?"

"What Richie thought important enough to tell you."

I grinned at him. "A week, maybe."

His eyes were deadly now. Cold behind the glasses, each one a deliberate ultimatum. "One week, then. No more. Try to go past it and I'll show you tricks you never thought of when it comes to making a man miserable."

"I could turn up the killer in that time."

"You won't."

"There were times when I didn't do so bad."

"Long ago, Hammer. Now you're nothing. Just don't mess anything up. The only reason I'm not pushing you hard is because you couldn't take the gaff. If I thought you could, my approach would be different."

I stood up and pushed my chair back. "Thanks for the consideration. I appreciate it."

"No trouble at all."

"I'll call you."

"Sure. I'll be waiting."

The same soft rain had come in again, laying a blanket over the city. It was gentle and cool, not heavy enough yet to send the sidewalk crowd into the bars or running for cabs. It was a good rain to walk in if you weren't in a hurry, a good rain to think in.

So I walked to Forty-fourth and turned west toward Broadway, following a pattern from seven years ago I had forgotten, yet still existed. At the Blue Ribbon I went into the bar, had a stein of Prior's dark beer, said hello to a few familiar faces, then went back toward the glow of lights that marked the Great White Way.

The night man in the Hackard Building was new to me, a sleepy-looking old guy who seemed to just be waiting time out so he could leave life behind and get comfortably dead. He watched me sign the night book, hobbled after me into the elevator and let me out where I wanted without a comment, anxious for nothing more than to get back to his chair on the ground floor.

I found my key, turned the lock and opened the door.

I was thinking of how funny it was that some things could transcend all others, how from the far reaches of your mind something would come, an immediate reaction to an immediate stimulus. I was thinking it and falling, knowing that I had been hit, but not hard, realizing that the cigarette smoke I smelled meant but one thing, that it wasn't mine, and if somebody were still there he had heard the elevator stop, had time to cut the lights and wait —and act. But time had not changed habit and my reaction was quicker than his act.

Metal jarred off the back of my head and bit into my neck. Even as I fell I could sense him turn the gun around in his hand and heard the click of a hammer going back. I hit face down, totally limp, feeling the warm spill of blood seeping into my collar. The light went on and a toe touched me gently. Hands felt my pockets, but it was a professional touch and the gun was always there and I couldn't move without being suddenly dead, and I had been dead too long already to invite it again.

The blood saved me. The cut was just big and messy enough to make him decide it was useless to push things any further. The feet stepped back, the door opened, closed, and I heard the feet walk away.

I got to the desk as fast as I could, fumbled out the .45, loaded it and wrenched the door open. The guy was gone. I knew he would be. He was long gone. Maybe I was lucky, because he was a real pro. He could have been standing there waiting, just in case, and his first shot would have gone right where he wanted it to. I looked at my hand and it was shaking too hard to put a bullet anywhere near a target. Besides, I had forgotten to jack a shell into the chamber. So some things did age with time, after all.

Except luck. I still had some of that left.

I walked around the office slowly, looking at the places that had been ravaged in a fine search for something. The shakedown had been fast, but again, in thoroughness, the marks of the complete professional were apparent. There had been no time or motion lost in the wrong direction and had I hidden anything of value that could have been tucked into an envelope, it would have been found. Two places I once considered original with me were torn open expertly, the second, and apparently last, showing a touch of annoyance.

Even Velda's desk had been torn open and the last thing she had written to me lay discarded on the floor, ground into a twisted sheet by a turning foot and all that was left was the heading.

It read, *Mike Darling*—and that was all I could see.

I grinned pointlessly, and this time I jacked a shell into the chamber and let the hammer ease down, then shoved the .45 into my belt on the left side. There was a sudden familiarity with the weight and the knowledge that here was life and death under my hand, a means of extermination, of quick vengeance, and of remembrance of the others who had gone down under that same gun.

Mike Darling—

Where was conscience when you saw those words?

Who *really* were the dead: those killing, or those already killed?

Then suddenly I felt like myself again and knew that the road back was going to be a long one alive or a short one dead and there wasn't even time enough to count the seconds.

Downstairs an old man would be dead in his chair because he alone could identify the person who came up here. The name in the night book would be fictitious and cleverly disguised if it had even been written there, and unless a motive were proffered, the old man's killing would be another one of those unexplainable things that happen to lonely people or alone people who stay too close to a terroristic world and are subject to the things that can happen by night.

I cleaned up the office so that no one could tell what had happened, washed my head and mopped up the blood spots on the floor, then went down the stairwell to the lobby.

The old man was lying dead in his seat, his neck broken neatly by a single blow. The night book was untouched, so his deadly visitor had only faked a signing. I tore the last page out, made sure I was unobserved and walked out the door. Someplace near Eighth Avenue I ripped up the page and fed the pieces into the gutter, the filthy trickle of rain-water swirling them into the sewer at the corner.

I waited until a cab came along showing its top light, whistled it over and told the driver where to take me. He hit the flag, pulled away from the curb and loafed his way down to the docks until he found the right place. He took his buck with another silent nod and left me there in front of Benny Joe Grissi's bar where you could get a program for all the trouble shows if you wanted one or a kill arranged or a broad made or anything at all you wanted just so long as you could get in the place.

But best of all, if there was anything you wanted to know about the stretch from the Battery to Grant's Tomb that constitutes New York's harbor facilities on either side of the river, or the associated unions from the NMU to the Teamsters, or wanted a name passed around the world, you could do it here. There was a place like it in London and Paris and Casablanca and Mexico City and Hong Kong and, if you looked hard enough, a smaller, more modified version would be in every city in the world. You just had to know where to look. And this was my town.

At the table near the door the two guys scrutinizing the customers made their polite sign which meant stay out. Then the little one got up rather tiredly and came over and said, "We're closing, buddy. No more customers."

When I didn't say anything he looked at my face and threw a finger toward his partner. The other guy was real big, his face suddenly ugly for having been disturbed. We got eye to eye and for a second he followed the plan and said, "No trouble, pal. We don't want trouble."

"Me either, kid."

"So blow."

I grinned at him, teeth all the way. "Scram."

My hand hit his chest as he swung and he went on his can swinging like an idiot. The little guy came in low, thinking he was pulling a good one, and I kicked his face all out of shape with one swipe and left him whimpering against the wall.

The whole bar had turned around by then, all talk ended. You could see the excitement in their faces, the way they all thought it was funny because somebody had nearly jumped the moat—but not quite. They were waiting to see the rest, like when the big guy got up off the floor and earned his keep and the big guy was looking forward to it too.

Out of the sudden quiet somebody said, "Ten to one on Sugar Boy," and, just as quietly, another one said, "You're on for five."

Again it was slow motion, the bar looking down at the funny little man at the end, wizened and dirty, but liking the odds, regardless of the company. Somebody laughed and said, "Pepper knows something."

"That I do," the funny little man said.

But by then the guy had eased up to his feet, his face showing how much he liked the whole deal, and just for the hell of it he let me have the first swing.

I didn't hurt him. He let me know it and came in like I knew he would and I was back in that old world since seven years ago, tasting floor dirt and gagging on it, feeling my guts fly apart and the wild wrenching of bones sagging under even greater bones and while they laughed and yelled at the bar, the guy slowly killed me until the little bit of light was there like I knew that would be too and I gave him the foot in the crotch and, as if the world had collapsed on his shoulders, he crumpled into a vomiting heap, eyes bulging, hating, waiting for the moment of incredible belly pain to pass, and when it did, reached for his belt and pulled out a foot-long knife and it was all over, all over for everybody because I reached too and no blade argues with that great big bastard of a .45 that makes the big boom so many times, and when he took one look at my face his eyes bulged again, said he was sorry, Mac, and to deal him out, I was the wrong guy, he knew it and don't let the boom go off. He was close for a second and knew it, then I put the gun back without letting the hammer down, stepped on the blade and broke it and told him to get up.

The funny little guy at the bar said, "That's fifty I got coming."

The one who made the bet said, "I told you Pepper knew something."

The big guy got up and said, "No offense, Mac, it's my job."

The owner came over and said, "Like in the old days, hey Mike?"

I said, "You ought to clue your help, Benny Joe."

"They need training."

"Not from me."

"You did lousy tonight. I thought Sugar Boy had you."

"Not when I got a rod."

"So who knew? All this time you go clean? I hear even

Gary Moss cleaned you one night. You, even. Old, Mike."

Around the bar the eyes were staring at me curiously, wondering. "They don't know me, Benny Joe."

The little fat man shrugged. "Who would? You got skinny. Now how about taking off."

"Not you, Benny Joe," I said, "Don't tell me you're pushing too."

"Sure. Tough guys I got all the time. Old tough guys I don't want. They always got to prove something. So with you I call the cops and you go down. So blow, okay?"

I hadn't even been looking at him while he talked, but now I took the time to turn around and see the little fat man, a guy I had known for fifteen years, a guy who should have known better, a guy who was on the make since he began breathing but a guy who had to learn the hard way.

So I looked at him, slow, easy, and in his face I could see my own face and I said, "How would you like to get deballed, Benny Joe? You got nobody to stop me. You want to sing tenor for that crib you have keeping house for you?"

Benny Joe almost did what he started out to do. The game was supposed to have ended in the Old West, the making of a reputation by one man taking down a big man. He almost took the .25 out, then he went back to being Benny Joe again and he was caught up in something too big for him. I picked the .25 out of his fingers, emptied it, handed it back and told him, "Don't die without cause, Benny Joe."

The funny little guy at the bar with the new fifty said, "You don't remember me, do you, Mike?"

I shook my head.

"Ten, fifteen years ago—the fire at Carrigan's?"

Again, I shook my head.

"I was a newspaperman then. Bayliss Henry of the *Telegram*. Pepper, they call me now. You had that gunfight with Cortez Johnson and his crazy bunch from Red Hook."

"That was long ago, feller."

"Papers said it was your first case. You had an assignment from Aliet Insurance."

"Yeah," I told him, "I remember the fire. Now I remember you too. I never did get to say thanks. I go through the whole damn war without a scratch and get hit in a lousy heist and almost burn to death. So thanks!"

"My pleasure, Mike. You got me a scoop bonus."

"Now what's new?"

"Hell, after what guys like us saw, what else *could* be new?"

I drank my beer and didn't say anything.

Bayliss Henry grinned and asked, "What's with you?"

"What?" I tried to sound pretty bored.

It didn't take with him at all. "Come on, Big Mike. You've always been my favorite news story. Even when I don't write, I follow the columns. Now you just don't come busting in this place anymore without a reason. How long were you a bum, Mike?"

"Seven years."

"Seven years ago you never would have put a gun on Sugar Boy."

"I didn't need it then."

"Now you need it?"

"Now I need it," I repeated.

Bayliss took a quick glance around. "You got no ticket for that rod, Mike."

I laughed, and my face froze him. "Neither had Capone. Was he worried?"

The others had left us. The two guys were back at their table by the door watching the rain through the windows, the music from the overlighted juke strangely soft for a change, the conversation a subdued hum above it.

A rainy night can do things like that. It can change the entire course of events. It seems to rearrange time.

I said, "What?"

"Jeez, Mike, why don't you listen once? I've been talking for ten minutes."

"Sorry, kid."

"Okay, I know how it is. Just one thing."

"What?"

"When you gonna ask it?"

I looked at him and took a pull of the beer.

"The big question. The one you came here to ask somebody."

"You think too much, Bayliss, boy."

He made a wry face. "I can think more. You got a big one on your mind. This is a funny place, like a thieves' market. Just anybody doesn't come here. It's a special place for special purposes. You want something, don't you?"

I thought a moment, then nodded. "What can you supply?"

His wrinkled face turned up to mine with a big smile. "Hell, man, for you just about anything."

"Know a man named Richie Cole?" I asked.

"Sure," he said, casually, "he had a room under mine. He was a good friend. A damn smuggler who was supposed to be small-time, but he was better than that because he had loot small smugglers never get to keep. Nice guy, though."

And that is how a leech line can start in New York if you know where to begin. The interweaving of events and personalities can lead you to a crossroad eventually where someone stands who, with one wave of a hand, can put you on the right trail—if he chooses to. But the interweaving is not a simple thing. It comes from years of mingling and mixing and kneading, and although the answer seems to be an almost casual thing, it really isn't at all.

I said, "He still live there?"

"Naw. He got another place. But he's no seaman."

"How do you know?"

Bayliss grunted and finished his beer. "Now what seaman will keep a furnished room while he's away?"

"How do you know this?"

The little guy shrugged and waved the bartender over. "Mike—I've been there. We spilled plenty of beer together." He handed me a fresh brew and picked up his own. "Richie Cole was a guy who made plenty of bucks, friend, and don't you forget it. You'd like him."

"Where's his place?"

Bayliss smiled broadly, "Come on, Mike. I said he was a friend. If he's in trouble I'm not going to make it worse."

"You can't," I told him. "Cole's dead."

Slowly, he put the beer down on the bar, turned and looked at me with his forehead wrinkling in a frown. "How?"

"Shot."

"You know something, Mike? I thought something like that would happen to him. It was in the cards."

"Like how?"

"I saw his guns. He had three of them in a trunk. Besides, he used me for a few things."

When I didn't answer, he grinned and shrugged.

"I'm an old-timer, Mike. Remember? Stuff I know hasn't been taught some of the fancy boys on the papers yet. I still got connections that get me a few bucks here and there. No trouble, either. I did so many favors that now it pays off and, believe me, this retirement pay business isn't what it looks like. So I pick up a few bucks with some well chosen directions or clever ideas. Now, Cole, I never did figure just what he was after, but he sure wanted some peculiar information."

"How peculiar?"

"Well, to a thinking man like me, it was peculiar because no smuggler the size he was supposed to be would want to know what he wanted."

"Smart," I told him. "Did you mention it to Cole?"

"Sure," Bayliss grinned, "but we're both old at what we were doing and could read eyes. I wouldn't pop on him."

"Suppose we go see his place."

"Suppose you tell me what he really was first."

Right then he was real roostery, a Bayliss Henry from years ago before retirement and top dog on the news beat, a wizened little guy, but one who wasn't going to budge an inch. I wasn't giving a damn for national security as the book describes it, at all, so I said, "Richie Cole was a

Federal agent and he stayed alive long enough to ask me in on this."

He waited, watched me, then made a decisive shrug with his shoulders and pulled a cap down over his eyes. "You know what you could be getting into?" he asked me.

"I've been shot before," I told him.

"Yeah, but you haven't been dead before," he said.

The place was a brownstone building in Brooklyn that stood soldier-fashion shoulder to shoulder in place with fifty others, a row of facelike oblongs whose windows made dull, expressionless eyes of the throttled dead, the bloated tongue of a stone stoop hanging out of its gaping mouth.

The rest wasn't too hard, not when you're city-born and have nothing to lose anyway. Bayliss said the room was ground-floor rear so we simply got into the back through a cellarway three houses down, crossed the slatted fences that divided one pile of garbage from another until we reached the right window, then went in. Nobody saw us. If they did, they stayed quiet about it. That's the kind of place it was.

In a finger-thick beam of the pencil flash I picked out the sofa bed, an inexpensive contour chair, a dresser and a desk. For a furnished room it had a personal touch that fitted in with what Bayliss suggested. There were times when Richie Cole had desired a few more of the creature comforts than he could normally expect in a neighborhood like this.

There were a few clothes in the closet; a military raincoat, heavy dungaree jacket and rough-textured shirts. An old pair of hip boots and worn high shoes were in one corner. The dresser held changes of underwear and a few sports shirts, but nothing that would suggest that Cole was anything he didn't claim to be.

It was in the desk that I found the answer. To anyone else it would have meant nothing, but to me it was an answer. A terribly cold kind of answer that seemed to come at me like a cloud that could squeeze and tear until I thought I was going to burst wide open.

Cole had kept a simple, inexpensive photo album. There were the usual pictures of everything from the Focking Distillery to the San Francisco Bridge with Cole and girls and other guys and girls and just girls alone the way a thousand other seamen try to maintain a visual semblance of life.

But it was in the first few pages of the album that the fist hit me in the gut because there was Cole a long time ago sitting at a table in a bar with some RAF types in the background and a couple of American GI's from the 8th Air Force on one side and with Richie Cole was Velda.

Beautiful, raven hair in a long pageboy, her breasts swelling tautly against the sleeveless gown, threatening to free themselves. Her lips were wet with an almost deliberate gesture and her smile was purposely designing. One of the GIs was looking at her with obvious admiration.

Bayliss whispered, "What'd you say, Mike?"

I shook my head and flipped a page over. "Nothing."

She was there again, and a few pages further on. Once they were standing outside a pub, posing with a soldier and a WREN, and in another they stood beside the bombed-out ruins of a building with the same soldier, but a different girl.

There was nothing contrived about the album. Those pictures had been there a long time. So had the letters. Six of them dated in 1944, addressed to Cole at a P.O. box in New York, and although they were innocuous enough in content, showed a long-standing familiarity between the two of them. And there was Velda's name, the funny "V" she made, the green ink she always used and, although I hadn't even known her then, I was hating Cole so hard it hurt. I was glad he was dead but wished I could have killed him, then I took a fat breath, held it once and let it out slowly and it wasn't so bad any more.

I felt Bayliss touch my arm and he said, "You okay, Mike?"

"Sure."

"You find anything?"

"Nothing important."

He grunted under his breath. "You're full of crap."

"A speciality of mine," I agreed. "Let's get out of here."

"What about those guns? He had a trunk some place."

"We don't need them. Let's go."

"So you found something. You could satisfy my curiosity."

"Okay," I told him, "Cole and I had a mutual friend."

"It means something?"

"It might. Now move."

He went out first, then me, and I let the window down. We took the same route back, going over the fences where we had crossed earlier, me boosting Bayliss up then following him. I was on top of the last one when I felt the sudden jar of wood beside my hand, then a tug at my coat between my arm and rib cage and the instinct and reaction grabbed me again and I fell on top of Bayliss while I hauled the .45 out and, without even knowing where the silenced shots were coming from, I let loose with a tremendous blast of that fat musket that tore the night wide open with a rolling thunder that let the world know the pigeon was alive and had teeth.

From a distance came a clattering of cans, of feet, then windows slammed open and voices started yelling and the two of us got out fast. We were following the same path of the one who had followed us, but his start was too great. Taillights were already diminishing down the street and in another few minutes a prowl car would be turning the corner.

We didn't wait for it.

Six blocks over we picked up a cab, drove to Ed Dailey's bar and got out. I didn't have to explain a thing to Bayliss. He had been through it all too often before. He was shaking all over and couldn't seem to stop swallowing. He had two double ryes before he looked at me with a peculiar expression and said softly, "Jeez, I'll never learn to keep my mouth shut."

Peerage Brokers could have been anything. The desks

and chairs and filing cabinets and typewriters represented nothing, yet represented everything. Only the gray man in the glasses sitting alone in the corner drinking coffee represented something.

Art Rickerby said, "Now?" and I knew what he meant.

I shook my head. He looked at me silently a moment, then sipped at the coffee container again. He knew how to wait, this one. He wasn't in a hurry now, not rushing to prevent something. He was simply waiting for a moment of vengeance because the thing was done and sooner or later time would be on his side.

I said, "Did you know Richie pretty well?"

"I think so."

"Did he have a social life?"

For a moment his face clouded over, then inquisitiveness replaced anger and he put the coffee container down for a reason, to turn his head away. "You'd better explain."

"Like girls," I said.

When he turned back he was expressionless again. "Richie had been married," he told me. "In 1949 his wife died of cancer."

"Oh? How long did he know her?"

"They grew up together."

"Children?"

"No. Both Richie and Ann knew about the cancer. They married after the war anyway but didn't want to leave any children a difficult burden."

"How about before that?"

"I understood they were both pretty true to each other."

"Even during the war?"

Again there was silent questioning in his eyes. "What are you getting at, Mike?"

"What was Richie during the war?"

The thought went through many channels before it was properly classified. Art said, "A minor O.S.I. agent. He was a Captain then based in England. With mutual understanding, I never asked, nor did he offer, the kind of work he did."

"Let's get back to the girls."

"He was no virgin, if that's what you mean."

He knew he reached me with that one but didn't know why. I could feel myself tighten up and had to relax deliberately before I could speak to him again.

"Who did he go with when he was here? When he wasn't on a job."

Rickerby frowned and touched his glasses with an impatient gesture. "There were—several girls. I really never inquired. After Ann's death—well, it was none of my business, really."

"But you knew them?"

He nodded, watching me closely. Once more he thought quickly, then decided. "There was Greta King, a stewardess with American Airlines that he would see occasionally. And there was Pat Bender over at the Craig House. She's a manicurist there and they had been friends for years. Her brother, Lester, served with Richie but was killed just before the war ended."

"It doesn't sound like he had much fun."

"He didn't look for fun. Ann's dying took that out of him. All he wanted was an assignment that would keep him busy. In fact, he rarely ever got to see Alex Bird, and if—"

"Who's he?" I interrupted.

"Alex, Lester and Richie were part of a team throughout the war. They were great friends in addition to being experts in their work. Lester got killed, Alex bought a chicken farm in Marlboro, New York, and Richie stayed in the service. When Alex went civilian he and Richie sort of lost communication. You know the code in this work—no friends, no relatives—it's a lonely life."

When he paused I said, "That's all?"

Once again, he fiddled with his glasses, a small flicker of annoyance showing in his eyes. "No. There was someone else he used to see on occasions. Not often, but he used to look forward to the visit."

My voice didn't sound right when I asked, "Serious?"

"I—don't think so. It didn't happen often enough and

generally it was just a supper engagement. It was an old friend, I think."

"You couldn't recall the name?"

"It was never mentioned. I never pried into his business."

"Maybe it's about time."

Rickerby nodded sagely. "It's about time for you to tell me a few things too."

"I can't tell you what I don't know."

"True." He looked at me sharply and waited.

"If the information isn't classified, find out what he really did during the war, who he worked with and who he knew."

For several seconds he ran the thought through his mental file, then: "You think it goes back that far?"

"Maybe." I wrote my number down on a memo pad, ripped off the page and handed it to him. "My office. I'll be using it from now on."

He looked at it, memorized it and threw it down. I grinned, told him so-long and left.

Over in the west Forties I got a room in a small hotel, got a box, paper and heavy cord from the desk clerk, wrapped my .45 up, addressed it to myself at the office with a buck's worth of stamps and dropped it in the outgoing mail, then sacked out until it was almost noon in a big new tomorrow.

Maybe I still had that look because they thought I was another cop. Nobody wanted to talk, and if they had, there would have been little they could have said. One garrulous old broad said she saw a couple of men in the back court and later a third. No, she didn't know what they were up to and didn't care as long as they weren't in *her* yard. She heard the shot and would show me the place, only she didn't know why I couldn't work with the rest of the cops instead of bothering everybody all over again.

I agreed with her, thanked her and let her take me to where I almost had it going over the fence. When she left, wheezing and muttering, I found where the bullet had torn through the slats and jumped the fence, and dug it out of the two-by-four frame in the section on the other side of the yard. There was still enough of it to show the rifling marks, so I dropped it in my pocket and went back to the street.

Two blocks away I waved down a cab and got in. Then I felt the seven years, and the first time back I had to play it hard and almost stupid enough to get killed. There was a time when I never would have missed with the .45, but now I was happy to make a noise with it big enough to start somebody running. For a minute I felt skinny and shrunken inside the suit and cursed silently to myself.

If she was alive, I was going to have to do better than I was doing now. Time, damn it. There wasn't any. It was like when the guy in the porkpie hat had her strung from the rafters and the whip in his hand had stripped her naked flesh with bright red welts, the force of each lash stroke making her spin so that the lush beauty of her body and the deep-space blackness of her hair and the wide sweep of her breasts made an obscene kaleidoscope and then I shot his arm off with the tommy gun and it dropped with a wet thud in the puddle of clothes around her feet like a pagan sacrifice and while he was dying I killed the rest of them, all of them, twenty of them, wasn't it? And they called me those terrible names, the judge and the jury did.

Damn. Enough.

CHAPTER 7

The body was gone, but the police weren't. The two detectives interrogating Nat beside the elevators were patiently listening to everything he said, scanning the night book one held open. I walked over, nodded and said, "Morning, Nat."

Nat's eyes gave me a half-scared, half-surprised look followed by a shrug that meant it was all out of his hands.

"Hello, Mike." He turned to the cop with the night book. "This is Mr. Hammer. In 808."

"Oh?" The cop made me in two seconds. "Mike Hammer. Didn't think you were still around."

"I just got back."

His eyes went up and down, then steadied on my face. He could read all the signs, every one of them. "Yeah," he said sarcastically. "Were you here last night?"

"Not me, buddy. I was out on the town with a friend."

The pencil came into his hand automatically. "Would you like to—"

"No trouble. Bayliss Henry, an old reporter. I think he lives—"

He put the pencil away with a bored air. "I know where Bayliss lives."

"Good," I said. "What's the kick here?"

88

Before the pair could tell him to shut up, Nat blurted, "Mike—it was old Morris Fleming. He got killed."

I played it square as I could. "Morris Fleming?"

"Night man, Mike. He started working here after—you left."

The cop waved him down. "Somebody broke his neck."

"What for?"

He held up the book. Ordinarily he never would have answered, but I had been around too long in the same business. "He could have been identified. He wanted in the easy way so he signed the book, killed the old man later and ripped the page out when he left." He let me think it over and added, "Got it figured yet?"

"You don't kill for fun. Who's dead upstairs?"

Both of them threw a look back and forth and stared at me again. "Clever boy."

"Well?"

"No bodies. No reported robberies. No signs of forcible entry. You're one of the last ones in. Maybe you'd better check your office."

"I'll do that," I told him.

But I didn't have to bother. My office had already been checked. Again. The door was open, the furniture pushed around, and in my chair behind the desk was Pat, his face cold and demanding, his hands playing with the box of .45 shells he had found in the niche in the desk.

Facing him with her back to me, the light from the window making a silvery halo around the yellow of her hair was Laura Knapp.

I said, "Having fun?"

Laura turned quickly, saw me and a smile made her mouth beautiful. "Mike!"

"Now how did you get here?"

She took my hand, held it tightly a moment with a grin of pleasure and let me perch on the end of the desk. "Captain Chambers asked me to." She turned and smiled at Pat, but the smile was lost on him. "He came to see me not long after you did."

"I told you that would happen."

"It seems that since you showed some interest in me he did too, so we just reviewed all—the details of what happened—to Leo." Her smile faded then, her eyes seeming to reflect the hurt she felt.

"What's the matter, Pat, don't you keep files any more?"

"Shut up."

"The manual says to be nice to the public." I reached over and picked up the box of .45's. "Good thing you didn't find the gun."

"You're damn right. You'd be up on a Sullivan charge right now."

"How'd you get in, Pat?"

"It wasn't too hard. I know the same tricks you do. And don't get snotty." He flipped a paper out of his pocket and tossed it on the desk. "A warrant, mister. When I heard there was a kill in this particular building I took this out first thing."

I laughed at the rage in his face and rubbed it in a little. "Find what you were looking for?"

Slowly, he got up and walked around the desk, and though he stood there watching me it was to Laura that he spoke. "If you don't mind, Mrs. Knapp, wait out in the other room. And close the door."

She looked at him, puzzled, so I nodded to her and she stood up with a worried frown creasing her eyes and walked out. The door made a tiny *snick* as it closed and we had the place all to ourselves. Pat's face was still streaked with anger, but there were other things in his eyes this time. "I'm fed up, Mike. You'd just better talk."

"And if I don't?"

The coldness took all the anger away from his face now. "All right, I'll tell you the alternative. You're trying to do something. Time is running against you. Don't give me any crap because I know you better than you know yourself. This isn't the first time something like this cropped up. You pull your connections on me, you try to play it smart —okay—I'll make time run out on you. I'll use every damn regulation I know to harass you to death. I'll keep a tail on you all day, and every time you spit I'll have your ass hauled into the office. I'll hold you on every pretext possible and if it comes to doing a little high-class framing I can do that too."

Pat wasn't lying. Like he knew me, I knew him. He was real ready to do everything he said and time was one thing I didn't have enough of. I got up and walked around the desk to my chair and sat down again. I pulled out the desk drawer, stowed the .45's back in the niche without trying to be smug about what I did with the gun. Then I sat there groping back into seven years, knowing that instinct went only so far, realizing that there was no time to relearn and that every line had to be straight across the corners.

I said, "Okay, Pat. Anything you want. But first a favor."

"No favors."

"It's not exactly a favor. It's an or else." I felt my face go as cold as his was. "Whether you like it or not I'm ready to take my chances."

He didn't answer. He couldn't. He was ready to throw his fist at my face again and would have, only he was too far away. Little by little he relaxed until he could speak, then all those years of being a cop took over and he shrugged, but he wasn't fooling me any. "What is it?"

"Nothing I couldn't do if I had the time. It's all a matter of public record."

He glanced at me shrewdly and waited.

"Look up Velda's P.I. license."

His jaw dropped open stupidly for a brief second, then snapped shut and his eyes followed suit. He stood there, knuckles white as they gripped the edge of the desk and he gradually leaned forward so that when he swung he wouldn't be out of reach this time.

"What kind of crazy stunt are you pulling?" His voice was almost hoarse.

I shook my head. "The New York State law says that you must have served three or more years in an accredited police agency, city, state, or federal in a rating of sergeant or higher to get a Private Investigator's license. It isn't easy to get and takes a lot of background work."

Quietly, Pat said, "She worked for you. Why didn't you ask?"

"One of the funny things in life. Her ticket was good enough for me at first. Later it never occurred to me to ask. I was always a guy concerned with the present anyway and you damn well know it."

"You bastard. What are you trying to pull?"

"Yes or no, Pat."

His grin had no humor in it. Little cords in his neck stood out against his collar and the pale blue of his eyes was deadly. "No," he said. "You're a wise guy, punk. Don't pull your tangents on me. You got this big feeling inside you that you're coming back at me for slapping you around. You're using *her* now as a pretty little oblique switch—but, mister, you're pulling your crap on the wrong soldier. You've just about had it, boy."

Before he could swing I leaned back in my chair with as much insolence as I could and reached in my pocket for the slug I had dug out of the fence. It was a first-class gamble, but not quite a bluff. I had the odds going for me and if I came up short, I'd still have a few hours ahead of him.

I reached out and laid the splashed-out bit of metal on the desk. "Don't *punk* me, man. Tell ballistics to go after that and tell me what I want and I'll tell you where that came from."

Pat picked it up, his mind putting ideas together, trying to make one thing fit another. It was hard to tell what he was thinking, but one thing took precedence over all others. He was a cop. First-rate. He wanted a killer. He had to play his own odds too.

"All right," he told me, "I can't take any chances. I don't get your point, but if it's a phony, you've had it."

I shrugged. "When will you know about the license?"

"It won't take long."

"I'll call you," I said.

He straightened up and stared out the window over my

head, still half in thought. Absently, he rubbed the back of his neck. "You do that," he told me. He turned away, putting his hat on, then reached for the door.

I stopped him. "Pat—"

"What?"

"Tell me something."

His eyes squinted at my tone. I think he knew what I was going to ask.

"Did you love Velda too?"

Only his eyes gave the answer, then he opened the door and left.

"May I come in?"

"Oh, Laura—please."

"Was there—trouble?"

"Nothing special." She came back to the desk and sat down in the client's chair, her face curious. "Why?"

With a graceful motion, she crossed her legs and brushed her skirt down over her knees. "Well, when Captain Chambers was with me—well, he spoke constantly of you. It was as if you were right in the middle of everything." She paused, turning her head toward me. "He hates you, doesn't he?"

I nodded. "But we were friends once."

Very slowly, her eyebrows arched. "Aren't most friendships only temporary at best?"

"That's being pretty cynical."

"No—only realistic. There are childhood friendships. Later those friends from school, even to the point of nearly blood brotherhood fraternities, but how long do they last? Are your Army or Navy friends still your friends or have you forgotten their names?"

I made a motion with my shoulders.

"Then your friends are only those you have at the moment. Either you outgrow them or something turns friendship into hatred."

"It's a lousy system," I said.

"But there it is, nevertheless. In 1945 Germany and Japan were our enemies and Russia and the rest our allies. Now our former enemies are our best friends and the former allies the direct enemies."

She was so suddenly serious I had to laugh at her. "Beautiful blondes aren't generally philosophers."

But her eyes didn't laugh back. "Mike—it really isn't that funny. When Leo was—alive, I attended to all his affairs in Washington. I still carry on, more or less. It's something he would have wanted me to do. I *know* how people who run the world think. I served cocktails to people making decisions that rocked the earth. I saw wars start over a drink and the friendship of generations between nations wiped out because one stupid, pompous political appointee wanted to do things his way. Oh, don't worry, I *know* about friendships."

"So this one went sour."

"It hurts you, doesn't it?"

"I guess so. It never should have happened that way."

"Oh?" For a few moments she studied me, then she knew. "The woman—we talked about—you both loved her?"

"I thought only I did." She sat there quietly then, letting me finish. "We both thought she was dead. He still thinks so and blames me for what happened."

"Is she, Mike?"

"I don't know. It's all very strange, but if there is even the most remote possibility that some peculiar thing happened seven years ago and that she is still alive somewhere, I want to know about it."

"And Captain Chambers?"

"He could never have loved her as I did. She was mine."

"If—you are wrong—and she is dead, maybe it would be better not to know."

My face was grinning again. Not me, just the face part. I stared at the wall and grinned idiotically. "If she is alive, I'll find her. If she is dead, I'll find who killed her. Then slowly, real slowly, I'll take him apart, inch by inch, joint by joint, until dying will be the best thing left for him."

I didn't realize that I was almost out of the chair, every muscle twisted into a monstrous spasm of murder. Then I felt her hands pulling me back and I let go and sat still until the hate seeped out of me.

"Thanks."

"I know what you feel like, Mike."

"You do?"

"Yes." Her hand ran down the side of my face, the fingers tracing a warm path along my jaw. "It's the way I felt about Leo. He was a great man, then suddenly for no reason at all he was dead."

"I'm sorry, Laura."

"But it's not over for me anymore, either."

I swung around in the chair and looked up at her. She was magnificent then, a study in symmetry, each curve of her wonderful body coursing into another, her face showing the full beauty of maturity, her eyes and mouth rich with color.

She reached out her hand and I stood up, tilted her chin up with my fingers and held her that way. "You're thinking, kitten."

"With you I have to."

"Why?"

"Because somehow you know Leo's death is part of her, and I feel the same way you do. Whoever killed Leo is going to die too."

I let go of her face, put my hands on her shoulders and pulled her close to me. "If he's the one I want I'll kill him for you, kid."

"No, Mike. I'll do it myself." And her voice was as cold and as full of purpose as my own when she said it. Then she added, "You just find that one for me."

"You're asking a lot, girl."

"Am I? After you left I found out all about you. It didn't take long. It was very fascinating information, but nothing I didn't know the first minute I saw you."

"That was me of a long time ago. I've been seven years drunk and I'm just over the bum stage now. Maybe I could drop back real easy. I don't know."

"I know."

"Nobody knows. Besides, I'm not authorized to pursue investigations."

"That doesn't seem to stop you."

A grin started to etch my face again. "You're getting to a point, kid."

She laughed gently, a full, quiet laugh. Once again her hand came up to my face. "Then I'll help you find your woman, Mike, if you'll find who killed Leo."

"Laura—"

"When Leo died the investigation was simply routine. They were more concerned about the political repercussions than in locating his killer. *They* forgot about that one, but I haven't. I thought I had, but I really hadn't. Nobody would look for me—they all promised and turned in reports, but they never really cared about finding that one. But you do, Mike, and somehow I know you will. Oh, you have no license and no authority, but I have money and it will put many things at your disposal. You take it. You find your woman, and while you're doing it, or before, or after, whatever you like, you find the one I want. Tomorrow I'll send you five thousand dollars in cash. No questions. No paperwork. No reports. Even if nothing comes of it there is no obligation on you."

Under my hands she was trembling. It didn't show on her face, but her shoulders quivered with tension. "You loved him very much," I stated.

She nodded. "As you loved her."

We were too close then, both of us feeling the jarring impact of new and sudden emotions. My hands were things of their own, leaving her shoulders to slide down to her waist, then reaching behind her to bring her body close to mine until it was touching, then pressing until a fusion was almost reached.

She had to gasp to breathe, and fingers that were light on my face were suddenly as fierce and demanding as my own as she brought me down to meet her mouth and the scalding touch of her tongue that worked serpentlike in a passionate orgy that screamed of release after so long a time.

She pulled away, her breasts moving spasmodically against my chest. Her eyes were wet and shimmering with a glow of disbelief that it could ever happen again and she said softly: "You, Mike—I want a man. It could never be anybody but—a man." She turned her eyes on mine, pleading. "Please, Mike."

"You never have to say please," I told her, then I kissed her again and we found our place in time and in distance, lost people who didn't have to hurry or be cautious and who could enjoy the sensual discomfort of a cold leather couch on naked skin and take pleasure in whispering of clothing and relish the tiny sounds of a bursting seam; two whose appetites had been stifled for much too long, yet who loved the food of flesh enough not to rush through the first offering, but to taste and become filled course by course until in an explosion of delight, the grand finale of the whole table, was served and partaken.

We were gourmets, the body satisfied, but the mind knowing that it was only a momentary filling and that there would be other meals, each different, each more succulent than the last in a never-ending progression of enjoyment. The banquet was over so we kissed and smiled at each other, neither having been the guest, but rather, one the host, the other the hostess, both having the same startling thought of *where was the past now? Could the present possibly be more important?*

When she was ready I said, "Let's get you home now, Laura."

"Must I?"

"You must."

"I could stay in town."

"If you did it would be a distraction I can't afford."

"But I live a hundred and ten miles from your city."

"That's only two hours up the Thruway and over the hills."

She grinned at me. "Will you come?"

I grinned back. "Naturally."

I picked up my hat and guided her to the outer office.

For a single, terrible moment I felt a wash of shame drench me with guilt. There on the floor where it had been squashed underfoot by the one who killed old Morris Fleming and who had taken a shot at me was the letter from Velda that began, *"Mike Darling—"*

We sat at the corner of the bar in P. J. Moriarty's steak and chop house on Sixth and Fifty-second and across the angle his eyes were terrible little beads, magnified by the lenses of his glasses. John, the Irish bartender, brought us each a cold Blue Ribbon, leaving without a word because he could feel the thing that existed there.

Art Rickerby said, "How far do you think you can go?"

"All the way," I said.

"Not with me."

"Then alone."

He poured the beer and drank it as if it were water and he was thirsty, yet in a perfunctory manner that made you realize he wasn't a drinker at all, but simply doing a job, something he had to do.

When he finished he put the glass down and stared at me blandly. "You don't realize just how alone you really are."

"I know. Now do we talk?"

"Do you?"

"You gave me a week, buddy."

"Uh-huh." He poured the rest of the bottle into the glass and made a pattern with the wet bottom on the bar. When he looked up he said, "I may take it back."

I shrugged. "So you found something out."

"I did. About you too."

"Go ahead."

From overhead, the light bounced from his glasses so I couldn't see what was happening to his eyes. He said, "Richie was a little bigger than I thought during the war. He was quite important. Quite."

"At his age?"

"He was your age, Mike. And during the war age can be as much of a disguise as a deciding factor."

"Get to it."

"My pleasure." He paused, looked at me and threw the rest of the beer down. "He commanded the Seventeen Group." When I didn't give him the reaction he looked for he asked me, "Did you ever hear of Butterfly Two?"

I covered the frown that pulled at my forehead by finishing my own beer and waving to John for another. "I heard of it. I don't know the details. Something to do with the German system of total espionage. They had people working for them ever since the First World War."

There was something like respect in his eyes now. "It's amazing that you even heard of it."

"I have friends in amazing places."

"Yes, you had."

As slowly as I could I put the glass down. "What's that supposed to mean?"

And then his eyes came up, fastened on my face so as not to lose sight of even the slightest expression and he said, "It was your girl, the one called Velda, that he saw on the few occasions he was home. She was something left over from the war."

The glass broke in my hand and I felt a warm surge of blood spill into my hand. I took the towel John offered me and held it until the bleeding stopped. I said, "Go on."

Art smiled. It was the wrong kind of smile, with a gruesome quality that didn't match his face. "He last saw her in Paris just before the war ended and at that time he was working on Butterfly Two."

I gave the towel back to John and pressed on the Band-Aid he gave me.

"Gerald Erlich was the target then. At the time his name wasn't known except to Richie—and the enemy. Does it make sense now?"

"No." My guts were starting to turn upside down. I reached for the beer again, but it was too much. I couldn't do anything except listen.

"Erlich was the head of an espionage ring that had

been instituted in 1920. Those agents went into every land in the world to get ready for the next war and even raised their children to be agents. Do you think World War II was simply the result of a political turnover?"

"Politics are not my speciality."

"Well, it wasn't. There was another group. It wasn't part of the German General Staff's machinations either. They utilized this group and so did Hitler—or better still, let's say vice versa."

I shook my head, not getting it at all.

"It was a world conquest scheme. It incorporated some of the greatest military and corrupt minds this world has ever known and is using global wars and brush-fire wars to its own advantage until one day when everything is ready *they* can take over the world for their own."

"You're nuts!"

"I am?" he said softly. "How many powers were involved in 1918?"

"All but a few."

"That's right. And in 1945?"

"All of them were—"

"Not quite. I mean, who were the major powers?"

"We were. England, Germany, Russia, Japan—"

"That narrows it down a bit, doesn't it? And now, right now, how many *major powers* are there really?"

What he was getting at was almost inconceivable. "Two. Ourselves and the Reds."

"Ah—now we're getting to the point. And they hold most of the world's land and inhabitants in their hands. They're the antagonists. They're the ones pushing and we're the ones holding."

"Damn it, Rickerby—"

"Easy, friend. Just think a little bit."

"Ah, think my ass. What the hell are you getting to? Velda's part of that deal? You have visions, man, you got the big bug! Damn, I can get better than that from them at a jag dance in the Village. Even the bearded idiots make more sense."

His mouth didn't smile. It twisted. "Your tense is unusual. You spoke as if she were alive."

I let it go. I deliberately played the beer into the glass until the head was foaming over the rim, then drank it off with a grimace of pleasure and put the glass down.

When I was ready I said, "So now the Reds are going to take over the world. They'll bury us. Well, maybe they will, buddy, but there won't be enough Reds around to start repopulating again, that's for sure."

"I didn't say that," Art told me.

His manner had changed again. I threw him an annoyed look and reached for the beer.

"I think the world conquest parties changed hands. The conqueror has been conquered. The Reds have located and are using this vast fund of information, this great organization we call Butterfly Two, and that's why the free world is on the defensive."

John asked me if I wanted another Blue Ribbon and I said yes. He brought two, poured them, put the bar check in the register and returned it with a nod. When he had gone I half swung around, no longer so filled with a crazy fury that I couldn't speak. I said, "You're lucky, Rickerby. I didn't know whether to belt you in the mouth or listen."

"You're fortunate you listened."

"Then finish it. You think Velda's part of Butterfly Two." Everything, yet nothing, was in his shrug. "I didn't ask that many questions. I didn't care. All I want is Richie's killer."

"That doesn't answer my question. What do you *think?*"

Once again he shrugged. "It looks like she was," he told me.

So I thought my way through it and let the line cut all the corners off because there wasn't that much time and I asked him, "What was Richie working on when he was killed?"

Somehow, he knew I was going to ask that one and shook his head sadly. "Not that at all. His current job had to do with illegal gold shipments."

"You're sure."

"I'm sure."

"Then what about this Erlich?"

Noncommittally, Art shrugged. "Dead or disappeared. Swallowed up in the aftermath of war. Nobody knows."

"Somebody does," I reminded him. "The Big Agency boys don't give up their targets that easily. Not if the target is so big it makes a lifetime speciality of espionage."

He reflected a moment and nodded. "Quite possible. However, it's more than likely Erlich is dead at this point. He'd be in his sixties now if he escaped the general round-up of agents after the war. When the underground organizations of Europe were free of restraint they didn't wait on public trials. They knew who their targets were and how to find them. You'd be surprised at just how many people simply disappeared, big people and little people, agents and collaborators both. Many a person we wanted badly went into a garbage pit somewhere."

"Is that an official attitude?"

"Don't be silly. We don't reflect on attitudes to civilians. Occasionally it becomes necessary—"

"Now, for instance," I interrupted.

"Yes, like now. And believe me, they're better off knowing nothing."

Through the glasses his eyes tried to read me, then lost whatever expression they had. There was a touch of contempt and disgust in the way he sat there, examining me like a specimen under glass, then the last part of my line cut across the last corner and I asked him casually, "Who's The Dragon?"

Art Rickerby was good. Damn, but he was good. It was as if I had asked what time it was and he had no watch. But he just wasn't that good. I saw all the little things happen to him that nobody else would have noticed and watched them grow and grow until he could contain them no longer and had to sluff them off with an aside remark. So with an insipid look that didn't become him at all he said, "Who?"

"Or is it whom? Art?"

I had him where the hair was short and he knew it. He had given me all the big talk but this one was one too big. It was even bigger than he was and he didn't quite know how to handle it. You could say this about him: he was a book man. He put all the facts through the machine in his head and took the risk alone. He couldn't tell what I knew, yet he couldn't tell what I didn't know. Neither could he take a chance on having me clam up.

Art Rickerby was strictly a statesman. A federal agent, true, a cop, a dedicated servant of the people, but foremost he was a statesman. He was dealing with big security now and all the wraps were off. We were in a bar drinking beer and somehow the world was at our feet. What was it Laura had said— *"I saw wars start over a drink—"* and now it was almost the same thing right here.

"You didn't answer me," I prodded.

He put his glass down, and for the first time his hand wasn't steady. "How did you know about that?"

"Tell me, is it a big secret?"

His voice had an edge to it. *"Top secret."*

"Well, whatta you know."

"Hammer—"

"Nuts, Rickerby. You tell me."

Time was on my side now. I could afford a little bit of it. He couldn't. He was going to have to get to a phone to let someone bigger than he was know that The Dragon wasn't a secret any longer. He flipped the mental coin and that someone lost. He turned slowly and took his glasses off, wiping them on a handkerchief. They were all fogged up. "The Dragon is a team."

"So is Rutgers."

The joke didn't go across. Ignoring it, he said, "It's a code name for an execution team. There are two parts, Tooth and Nail."

I turned the glass around in my hand, staring at it, waiting. I asked, "Commies?"

"Yes." His reluctance was almost tangible. He finally said, "I can name persons throughout the world in critical positions in government who have died lately, some violently, some of natural causes apparently. You would probably recognize their names."

"I doubt it. I've been out of circulation for seven years."

He put the glasses on again and looked at the backbar. "I wonder," he mused to himself.

"The Dragon, Rickerby, if it were so important, how come the name never appeared. With a name like that it was bound to show."

"Hell," he said, "it was *our* code name, not theirs." His hands made an innocuous gesture, then folded together. "And now that you know something no one outside our agency knows, perhaps you'll tell *me* a little something about The Dragon."

"Sure," I said, and I watched his face closely. "The Dragon killed Richie."

Nothing showed.

"Now The Dragon is trying to kill Velda."

Still nothing showed, but he said calmly, "How do you know?"

"Richie told me. That's what he told me before he died. So she couldn't be tied up with the other side, could she?"

Unexpectedly, he smiled, tight and deadly and you really couldn't tell what he was thinking. "You never know," Art answered. "When their own kind slip from grace, they too become targets. We have such in our records. It isn't even unusual."

"You bastard."

"You know too much, Mr. Hammer. You might become a target yourself."

"I wouldn't be surprised."

He took a bill from his pocket and put it on the bar. John took it, totaled up the check and hit the register. When he gave the change back Art said, "Thanks for being so candid. Thank you for The Dragon."

"You leaving it like that?"

"I think that's it, don't you?"

"Sucker," I said.

He stopped halfway off his stool.

"You don't think I'd be that stupid, do you? Even after seven years I wouldn't be that much of a joker."

For a minute he was the placid little gray man I had first met, then almost sorrowfully he nodded and said, "I'm losing my insight. I thought I had it all. What else do you know?"

I took a long pull of the Blue Ribbon and finished the glass. When I put it down I said to him, "Richie told me something else that could put his killer in front of a gun."

"And just what is it you want for this piece of information?"

"Not much," I grinned. "Just an official capacity in some department or another so that I can carry a gun."

"Like in the old days," he said.

"Like in the old days," I repeated.

CHAPTER 8

Hy Gardner was taping a show and I didn't get to see him until it was over. We had a whole empty studio to ourselves, the guest chairs to relax in and for a change a quiet that was foreign to New York.

When he lit his cigar and had a comfortable wreath of smoke over his head he said, "How's things going, Mike?"

"Looking up. Why, what have you heard?"

"A little here and there," he shrugged. "You've been seen around." Then he laughed with the cigar in his teeth and put his feet up on the coffee table prop. "I heard about the business down in Benny Joe Grissi's place. You sure snapped back in a hurry."

"Hell, I don't have time to train. Who put you on the bit?"

"Old Bayliss Henry still has his traditional afternoon drink at Ted's with the rest of us. He knew we were pretty good friends."

"What did he tell you?"

Hy grinned again. "Only about the fight. He knew that would get around. I'd sooner hear the rest from you anyway."

"Sure."

"Should I tape notes?"

"Not yet. It's not that big yet, but you can do something for me."

"Just say it."

"How are your overseas connections?"

Hy took the cigar out, studied it and knocked off the ash. "I figure the next question is going to be a beauty."

"It is."

"Okay," he nodded. "In this business you have to have friends. Reporters aren't amateurs, they have sources of information and almost as many ways of getting what they want as Interpol has."

"Can you code a request to your friends and get an answer back the same way?"

After a moment he nodded.

"Swell. Then find out what anybody knows about The Dragon."

The cigar went back, he dragged on it slowly and let out a thin stream of smoke.

I said, "That's a code name too. Dragon is an execution team. Our side gave it the tag and it's a top secret bit, but that kind of stew is generally the easiest to stir once you take the lid off the kettle."

"You don't play around, do you?"

"I told you, I haven't got time."

"Damn, Mike, you're really sticking it out, aren't you?"

"You'll get the story."

"I hope you're alive long enough to give it to me. The kind of game you're playing has put a lot of good men down for keeps."

"I'm not exactly a patsy," I said.

"You're not the same Mike Hammer you were either, friend."

"When can you get the information off?" I asked him.

"Like now," he told me.

There was a pay phone in the corridor outside. The request went through Bell's dial system to the right party and the relay was assured. The answer would come into Hy's office at the paper coded within a regular news trans-

mission and the favor was expected to be returned when
needed.

Hy hung up and turned around. "Now what?"

"Let's eat, then take a run down to the office of a cop
who used to be a friend."

I knocked and he said to come in and when he saw
who it was his face steeled into an expression that was
so noncommittal it was pure betrayal. Behind it was all
the resentment and animosity he had let spew out earlier,
but this time it was under control.

Dr. Larry Snyder was sprawled out in a wooden desk
chair left over from the gaslight era, a surprised smile
touching the corner of his mouth as he nodded to me.

I said, "Hy Gardner, Dr. Larry Snyder. I think you
know Pat Chambers."

"Hi, Larry. Yes, I know Captain Chambers."

They nodded all around, the pleasantries all a fat fake,
then Hy took the other chair facing the desk and sat down.
I just stood there looking down at Pat so he could know
that I didn't give a damn for him either if he wanted it
that way.

Pat's voice had a cutting edge to it and he took in Hy
with a curt nod. "Why the party?"

Hy's got an interest in the story end."

"We have a procedure for those things."

"Maybe you have, but I don't and this is the way it's
going to be, old buddy."

"Knock it off."

Quietly, Larry said, "Maybe it's a good thing I brought
my medical bag, but if either one of you had any sense
you'd keep it all talk until you find the right answers."

"Shut up, Larry," Pat snarled, "you don't know anything about this."

"You'd be surprised at what I know," he told him. Pat
let his eyes drift to Larry's and he frowned. Then all
his years took hold and his face went blank again.

I said, "What did ballistics come up with?"

He didn't answer me and didn't have to. I knew by his

silence that the slug matched the others. He leaned on the desk, his hands folded together and when he was ready he said, "Okay, where did you get it?"

"We had something to trade, remember?"

His grin was too crooked. "Not necessarily."

But my grin was just as crooked. "The hell it isn't. Time isn't working against me any more, kiddo. I can hold out on you as long as I feel like it."

Pat half started to rise and Larry said cautioningly, "Easy, Pat."

He let out a grunt of disgust and sat down again. In a way he was like Art, always thinking, but covering the machinery of his mind with clever little moves. But I had known Pat too long and too well. I knew his play and could read the signs. When he handed me the photostat I was smiling even dirtier and he let me keep on with it until I felt the grin go tight as a drum, then pull into a harsh grimace. When I looked at Pat his face mirrored my own, only his had hate in it.

"Read it out loud," he said.

"Drop dead."

"No," he insisted, his voice almost paternal, a woodshed voice taking pleasure in the whipping, "go ahead and read it."

Silently, I read it again. Velda had been an active agent for the O.S.I. during the war, certain code numbers in the Washington files given for reference, and her grade and time in that type of service had qualified her for a Private Investigator's ticket in the State of New York.

Pat waited, then finally, "Well?"

I handed back the photostat. It was my turn to shrug, then I gave him the address in Brooklyn where Cole had lived and told him where he could find the hole the slug made. I wondered what he'd do when he turned up Velda's picture.

He let me finish, picked up the phone and dialed an extension. A few minutes later another officer laid a folder on his desk and Pat opened it to scan the sheet inside. The first report was enough. He closed the folder and rocked back in the chair. "There were two shots. They didn't come from the same gun. One person considered competent said the second was a large-bore gun, most likely a .45."

"How about that," I said.

His eyes were tight and hard now. "You're being cute, Mike. You're playing guns again. I'm going to catch you at it and then your ass is going to be hung high. You kill anybody on this prod and I'll be there to watch them strap you in the hot squat. I could push you a little more on this right now and maybe see you take a fall, but if I do it won't be enough to satisfy me. When you go down, I want to see you fall all the way, a six-foot fall like the man said."

"Thanks a bunch."

"No trouble," he smiled casually.

I glanced at Larry, then nodded toward Pat. "He's a sick man, Doctor. He won't admit it, but he *was* in love with her too."

Pat's expression didn't change a bit.

"Weren't you?" I asked him.

He waited until Hy and I were at the door and I had turned around to look at him again and this time I wasn't going to leave until he had answered me. He didn't hesitate. Softly, he said, "Yes, damn you."

On the street Hy steered me toward a bar near the Trib Building. We picked a booth in the back, ordered a pair of frigid Blue Ribbons and toasted each other silently when they came. Hy said, "I'm thinking like Alice in Wonderland now, that things keep getting curiouser and curiouser. You've given me a little bit and now I want more. It's fun writing a Broadway column and throwing out squibs about famous people and all that jazz, but essentially I'm a reporter and it wouldn't feel bad at all to do a little poking and prying again for a change.

"I don't know where to start, Hy."

"Well, give it a try."

"All right. How about this one. *Butterfly Two, Gerald Erlich.*"

The beer stopped halfway to his mouth. "How did you know about Butterfly Two?"

"How did *you* know about it?"

"That's war stuff, friend. Do you know what I was then?"

"A captain in special services, you told me."

"That's right. I was. But it was a cover assignment at times too. I was also useful in several other capacities besides."

"Don't tell me you were a spy."

"Let's say I just kept my ear to the ground regarding certain activities. But what's this business about Butterfly Two and Erlich? That's seventeen years old now and out of style."

"Is it?"

"Hell, Mike, when that Nazi war machine——" then he got the tone of my voice and put the glass down, his eyes watching me closely. "Let's have it, Mike."

"Butterfly Two isn't as out of style as you think."

"Look——"

"And what about Gerald Erlich?"

"Presumed dead."

"Proof?"

"None, but damn it, Mike——"

"Look, there are too many suppositions."

"What are you driving at, anyway? Man, don't tell me about Gerald Erlich. I had contact with him on three different occasions. The first two I knew him only as an allied officer, the third time I saw him in a detention camp after the war but didn't realize who he was until I went over it in my mind for a couple of hours. When I went back there the prisoners had been transferred and the truck they were riding in had hit a land mine taking a detour around a bombed bridge. It was the same truck Giesler was on, the SS Colonel who had all the prisoners killed during the Battle of the Bulge."

"You saw the body?"

"No, but the survivors were brought in and he wasn't among them."

"Presumed dead?"

"What else do you need? Listen, I even have a picture of the guy I took at that camp and some of those survivors when they were brought back. He wasn't in that bunch at all."

I perched forward on my chair, my hands flat on the table. "You have *what?*"

Surprised at the edge in my voice, he pulled out another one of those cigars. "They're in my personal stuff upstairs." He waved a thumb toward the street.

"Tell me something, Hy," I said, "Are you cold on these details?"

He caught on quick. "When I got out of the army, friend, I got out. All the way. I was never that big that they called me back as a consultant."

"Can we see those photos?"

"Sure. Why not?"

I picked up my beer, finished it, waited for him to finish his, then followed him out. We went back through the press section of the paper, took the service elevator up and got out at Hy's floor. Except for a handful of night men, the place was empty, a gigantic echo chamber that magnified the sound of our feet against the tiled floor. Hy unlocked his office, flipped on the light and pointed to a chair.

It took him five minutes of rummaging through his old files, but he finally came up with the photos. They were 120 contact sheets still in a military folder that was getting stiff and yellow around the edges and when he laid them out he pointed to one in the top left-hand corner and gave me an enlarging glass to bring out the image.

His face came in loud and clear, chunky features that bore all the physical traits of a soldier with overtones of one used to command. The eyes were hard, the mouth a tight slash as they looked contemptuously at the camera.

Almost as if he knew what was going to happen, I thought.

Unlike the others, there was no harried expression, no trace of fear. Nor did he have the stolid composure of a prisoner. Again, it was as if he were not really a prisoner at all.

Hy pointed to the shots of the survivors of the accident. He wasn't in any of those. The mangled bodies of the dead were unrecognizable.

Hy said, "Know him?"

I handed the photos back. "No."

"Sure?"

"I never forget faces."

"Then that's one angle out."

"Yeah," I said.

"But where did you ever get hold of that bit?"

I reached for my hat. "Have you ever heard of a red herring?"

Hy chuckled and nodded. "I've dropped a few in my life."

"I think I might have picked one up. It stinks."

"So drop it. What are you going to do now?"

"Not drop it, old buddy. It stinks just a little too bad to be true. No, there's another side to this Erlich angle I'd like to find out about."

"Clue me."

"Senator Knapp."

"The Missile Man, Mr. America. Now how does he come in?"

"He comes in because he's dead. The same bullet killed him as Richie Cole and the same gun shot at me. That package on Knapp that you gave me spelled out his war record pretty well. He was a light colonel when he went in and a major general when he came out. I'm wondering if I could tie his name in with Erlich's anyplace."

Hy's mouth came open and he nearly lost the cigar. *"Knapp working for another country?"*

"Hell no," I told him. "Were you?"

"But—"

"He could have had a cover assignment too."

"For Pete's sake, Mike, if Knapp had a job other than

what was known he could have made political capital of it and—"

"Who knew about yours?"

"Well—nobody, naturally. At least, not until now," he added.

"No friends?"

"No."

"Only authorized personnel."

"Exactly. And they were mighty damn limited."

"Does Marilyn know about it now?"

"Mike—"

"Does she?"

"Sure, I told her one time, but all that stuff is seventeen years old. She listened politely like a wife will, made some silly remark and that was it."

"The thing is, she knows about it."

"Yes. So what?"

"Maybe Laura Knapp does too."

Hy sat back again, sticking the cigar in his mouth. "Boy," he said, "you sure are a cagy one. You'll rationalize anything just to see that broad again, won't you?"

I laughed back at him. "Could be," I said. "Can I borrow that photo of Erlich?"

From his desk Hy pulled a pair of shears, cut out the shot of the Nazi agent and handed it to me. "Have fun, but you're chasing a ghost now."

"That's how it goes. But at least if you run around long enough something will show up."

"Yeah, like a broad."

"Yeah," I repeated, then reached for my hat and left.

Duck-Duck Jones told me that they had pulled the cop off Old Dewey's place. A relative had showed up, some old dame who claimed to be his half sister and had taken over Dewey's affairs. The only thing she couldn't touch was the newsstand which he had left to Duck-Duck in a surprise letter held by Bucky Harris who owned the Clover Bar. Even Duck-Duck could hardly believe it, but now pride of ownership had taken hold and he was happy to take up where the old man left off.

When I had his ear I said, "Listen, Duck-Duck, before Dewey got bumped a guy left something with him to give to me."

"Yeah? Like what, Mike?"

"I don't know. A package or something. Maybe an envelope. Anyway, did you see anything laying around here with my name on it? Or just an unmarked thing."

Duck folded a paper and thrust it at a customer, made change and turned back to me again. "I don't see nuttin', Mike. Honest. Besides, there ain't no place to hide nuttin' here. You wanna look around?"

I shook my head. "Naw, you would have found it by now."

"Well what you want I should do if somethin' shows up?"

"Hang onto it, Duck. I'll be back." I picked up a paper and threw a dime down.

I started to leave and Duck stopped me. "Hey, Mike, you still gonna do business here? Dewey got you down for some stuff."

"You keep me on the list, Duck. I'll pick up everything in a day or two."

I waved, waited for the light and headed west across town. It was a long walk, but at the end of it was a guy who owed me two hundred bucks and had the chips to pay off on the spot. Then I hopped a cab to the car rental agency on Forty-ninth, took my time about picking out a Ford coupé and turned toward the West Side Drive.

It had turned out to be a beautiful day, it was almost noon, the sun was hot, and once on the New York Thruway I had the wide concrete road nearly to myself. I stayed at the posted sixty and occasionally some fireball would come blasting by, otherwise it was smooth run with only a few trucks to pass. Just before I reached Harriman I saw the other car behind me close to a quarter mile and hold there. Fifteen miles further at the Newburgh entrance it was still there so I stepped it up to

seventy. Momentarily, the distance widened, then closed
and we stayed like that. Then just before the New Paltz
exit the car began to close the gap, reached me, passed
and kept on going. It was a dark blue Buick Special with a
driver lazing behind the wheel and as he went by all the
tension left my shoulders. What he had just pulled was
a typical tricky habit of a guy who had driven a long way
—staying behind a car until boredom set in, then running
for it to find a new pacer for a while. I eased off back
to sixty, turned through the toll gate at Kingston, picked
up Route 28 and loafed my way up to the chalet called
The Willows and when I cut the motor of the car I could
hear music coming through the trees from behind the
house and knew that she was waiting for me.

She was lying in the grass at the edge of the pool,
stretched out on an oversize towel with her face cradled
in her intertwined fingers. Her hair spilled forward over
her head, letting the sun tan her neck, her arms pulled
forward so that lines of muscles were in gentle bas-relief
down her back into her hips. Her legs were stretched
wide in open supplication of the inveterate sun worshipper
and her skin glistened with a fine, golden sweat.

Beside her the shortwave portable boomed in a sym-
phony, the thunder of it obliterating any sound of my
feet. I sat there beside her, quietly, looking at the beauty
of those long legs and the pert way her breasts flattened
against the towel, and after long minutes passed the music
became muted and drifted off into a finale of silence.

I said, "Hello, Laura," and she started as though suddenly awakened from sleep, then realizing the state of
affairs, reached for the edge of the towel to flip it around
her. I let out a small laugh and did it for her.

She rolled over, eyes wide, then saw me and laughed
back. "Hey, you."

"You'll get your tail burned lying around like that."

"It's worse having people sneak up on you."

I shrugged and tucked my feet under me. "It was worth
it. People like me don't get to see such lovely sights very
often."

Her eyes lit up impishly. "That's a lie. Besides, I'm not that new to you," she reminded me.

"Out in the sunlight you are, kitten. You take on an entirely new perspective."

"Are you making love or being clinical?" she demanded.

"I don't know. One thing could lead into another."

"Then maybe we should just let nature take its course."

"Maybe."

"Feel like a swim."

"I didn't bring a suit."

"Well . . ." and she grinned again.

I gave her a poke in the ribs with my forefinger and she grunted. "There are some things I'm prudish about, baby."

"Well I'll be damned," she whispered in amazement. "You never can tell, can you?"

"Sometimes never."

"There are extra suits in the bathhouse."

"That sounds better."

"Then let me go get into one first. I'm not going to be all skin while you play coward."

I reached for her but she was too fast, springing to her feet with the rebounding motion of a tumbler. She swung the towel sari-fashion around herself and smiled, knowing she was suddenly more desirable then than when she was naked. She let me eat her with my eyes for a second, then ran off boyishly, skirting the pool, and disappeared into the dressing room on the other side.

She came back out a minute later in the briefest black bikini I had ever seen, holding up a pair of shorts for me. She dropped them on a chair, took a run for the pool and dove in. I was a nut for letting myself feel like a colt, but the day was right, the woman was right and those seven years had been a long, hard grind. I walked over, picked up the shorts and without bothering to turn on the overhead light got dressed and went back out to the big, big day.

Underwater she was like an eel, golden brown, the black of the bikini making only the barest slashes against her skin. She was slippery and luscious and more tantaliz-

ing than a woman had a right to be. She surged up out
of the water and sat on the edge of the pool with her
stomach sucked in so that a muscular valley ran from her
navel up into the cleft of her breasts whose curves arched
up in proud nakedness a long way before feeling the
constraint of the miniature halter.

She laughed, stuck her tongue out at me and walked
to the grass by the radio and sat down. I said, "Damn,"
softly, waited a bit, then followed her.

When I was comfortable she put her hand out on mine,
making me seem almost prison-pale by comparison. "Now
we can talk, Mike. You didn't come all the way up here
just to see me, did you?"

"I didn't think so before I left."

She closed her fingers over my wrist. "Can I tell you
something very frankly?"

"Be my guest."

"I like you, big man."

I turned my head and nipped at her forearm. "The
feeling's mutual, big girl. It shouldn't be though."

"Why not?" Her eyes were steady and direct, deep and
warm as they watched and waited for the answer.

"Because we're not at all alike. We're miles apart in
the things we do and the way we think. I'm a trouble
character, honey. It's always been that way and it isn't
going to change. So be smart. Don't encourage me because
I'll only be too anxious to get in the game. We had a
pretty hello and a wonderful beginning and I came up here
on a damn flimsy pretext because I was hungry for you
and now that I've had a taste again I feel like a pig and
want it all."

"Ummmm," Laura said.

"Don't laugh," I told her. "White eyes is not speaking
with forked tongue. This old soldier has been around."

"There and back?"

"All the way, buddy."

Her grin was the kind they paint on pixie dolls. "Okay,
old soldier, so kill me."

"It'll take days and days."

"Ummm," she said again. "But tell m₃ your pretext for coming in the first place."

I reached out and turned the radio down. "It's about Leo."

The smile faded and her eyes crinkled at the corners. "Oh?"

"Did he ever tell you about his—well, job let's say, during the war?"

She didn't seem certain of what I asked. "Well, he was a general. He was on General Stoeffler's staff."

"I know that. But what did he *do?* Did he ever speak about what his job was?"

Again, she looked at me, puzzled. "Yes. Procurement was their job. He never went into great detail and I always thought it was because he never saw any direct action. He seemed rather ashamed of the fact."

I felt myself make a disgusted face.

"Is there—anything specific—like—"

"No," I said bluntly, "it's just that I wondered if he could possibly have had an undercover job."

"I don't understand, Mike." She propped herself up on one elbow and stared at me. "Are you asking if Leo was part of the cloak-and-dagger set?"

I nodded.

The puzzled look came back again and she moved her head in easy negative. "I think I would have known. I've seen all his old personal stuff from the war, his decorations, his photos, his letters of commendation and heard what stories he had to tell. But as I said, he always seemed to be ashamed that he wasn't on the front line getting shot at. Fortunately, the country had a better need for him."

"It was a good try," I said and sat up.

"I'm sorry, Mike."

Then I thought of something, told her to wait and went back to the bathhouse. I got dressed and saw the disappointment in her eyes from all the way arcoss the pool when I came out, but the line had to be drawn someplace.

Laura gave me a look of mock disgust and patted the

grass next to her. When I squatted down I took out the photo of Gerald Erlich and passed it over. "Take a look, honey. Have you ever seen that face in any of your husband's effects?"

She studied it, her eyes squinting in the sun, and when she had made sure she handed it back. "No, I never have. Who is he?"

"His name used to be Gerald Erlich. He was a trained espionage agent working for the Nazis during the war."

"But what did he have to do with Leo?"

"I don't know," I told her. "His name has been coming up a little too often to be coincidental."

"Mike—" She bit her lip, thinking, then: "I have Leo's effects in the house. Do you think you might find something useful in them? They might make more sense to you than they do to me."

"It sure won't hurt to look." I held out my hand to help her up and that was as far as I got. The radio between us suddenly burst apart almost spontaneously and slammed backward into the pool.

I gave her a shove that threw her ten feet away, rolled the other way and got to my feet running like hell for the west side of the house. It had to have been a shot and from the direction the radio skidded I could figure the origin. It had to be a silenced blast from a pistol because a rifle would have had either Laura or me with no trouble at all. I skirted the trees, stopped and listened, and from almost directly ahead I heard a door slam and headed for it wishing I had kept the .45 on me and to hell with Pat. The bushes were too thick to break through so I had to cut down the driveway, the gravel crunching under my feet. I never had a chance. All I saw was the tail end of a dark blue Buick special pulling away to make a turn that hid it completely.

And now the picture was coming out a little clearer. It hadn't been a tired driver on the Thruway at all. The bastard had picked me up at Duck's stand, figured he had given me something when he had handed me the paper, probably hired a car the same time I did with plenty of time to do it in since I wasn't hurrying at all. He followed me until he was sure he knew where I was headed and waited me out.

Damn. It was too close. But what got me was, how many silenced shots had he fired before hitting that radio? He had been too far away for accurate shooting apparently, but he could have been plunking them all around us hoping for a hit until he got the radio. Damn!

And I was really important. He knew where I was heading. Even since I had started to operate I had had a tail on me and it had almost paid off for him. But if I were important dead, so was Laura, because now that killer could never be sure I hadn't let her in on the whole business. Another damn.

She stood over the wreckage of the portable she had fished from the pool, white showing at the corners of her mouth. Her hands trembled so that she clasped them in front of her and she breathed as though she had done the running, not me. Breathlessly, she said, "Mike—what was it? Please, Mike—"

I put my arm around her shoulder and with a queer sob she buried her face against me. When she looked up she had herself under control. "It was a shot, wasn't it?"

"That's right. A silenced gun."

"But—"

"It's the second time he's tried for me."

"Do you think—"

"He's gone for now," I said.

"But who was he?"

"I think he was The Dragon, sugar."

For a few seconds she didn't answer, then she turned her face up toward mine. "Who?"

"Nobody you know. He's an assassin. Up until now his record has been pretty good. He must be getting the jumps."

"My gracious, Mike, this is crazy! It's absolutely crazy."

I nodded in agreement. "You'll never know, but now we have a real problem. You're going to need protection."

"Me!"

"Anybody I'm close to is in trouble. The best thing we can do is call the local cops."

She gave me a dismayed glance. "But I can't—I have to be in Washington— Oh, Mike!"

"It won't be too bad in the city, kid, but out here you're too alone."

Laura thought about it, then shrugged. "I suppose you're right. After Leo was killed the police made me keep several guns handy. In fact, there's one in each room."

"Can you use them?"

Her smile was wan. "The policeman you met the last time showed me."

"Swell, but what about out here?"

"There's a shotgun in the corner of the bathhouse."

"Loaded?"

"Yes."

"A shotgun isn't exactly a handgun."

"Leo showed me how to use it. We used to shoot skeet together at the other end of the property."

"Police protection would still be your best bet."

"Can it be avoided?"

"Why stick your neck out?"

"Because from now on I'm going to be a very busy girl, Mike. Congress convenes this week and the race is on for hostess of the year."

"That stuff is a lot of crap."

"Maybe, but that's what Leo wanted."

"So he's leaving a dead hand around."

There was a hurt expression on her face. "Mike—I did love him. Please . . .?"

"Sorry, kid. I don't have much class. We bat in different leagues."

She touched me lightly, her fingers cool. "Perhaps not. I think we are really closer than you realize."

I grinned and squeezed her hand, then ran my palm along the soft swell of her flanks.

Laura smiled and said, "Are you going to—do anything about that shot?"

"Shall I?"

"It's up to you. This isn't my league now."

I made the decision quickly. "All right, we'll keep it quiet. If that slob has any sense he'll know we won't be stationary targets again. From now on I'll be doing some hunting myself."

"You sure, Mike?"

"I'm sure."

"Good. Then let's go through Leo's effects."

Inside she led me upstairs past the bedrooms to the end of the hall, opened a closet and pulled out a small trunk. I took it from her, carried it into the first bedroom and dumped the contents out on the dresser.

When you thought about it, it was funny how little a man actually accumulated during the most important years of his life. He could go through a whole war, live in foreign places with strange people, be called upon to do difficult and unnatural work, yet come away from those years with no more than he could put in a very small trunk.

Leo Knapp's 201 file was thick, proper and as military as could be. There was an attempt at a diary that ran into fifty pages, but the last third showed an obvious effort being made to overcome boredom, then the thing dwindled out. I went through every piece of paperwork there was, uncovering nothing, saving the photos until last.

Laura left me alone to work uninterruptedly, but the smell of her perfume was there in the room and from somewhere downstairs I could hear her talking on the phone. She was still tense from the experience outside and although I couldn't hear her conversation I could sense the strain in her voice. She came back in ten minutes later and sat on the edge of the bed, quiet, content just to be there, then she sighed and I knew the tension had gone out of her.

I don't know what I expected, but the results were a total negative. Of the hundreds of photos, half were taken by G.I. staff photogs and the rest an accumulation of camp and tourist shots that every soldier who ever came home had tucked away in his gear. When you were old and fat you could take them out, reminisce over the days when you were young and thin and wonder what had happened to all the rest in the picture before putting them back in storage for another decade.

Behind me Laura watched while I began putting things back in the trunk and I heard her ask, "Anything, Mike?"

"No." I half threw his medals in the pile. "Everything's as mundane as a mud pie."

"I'm sorry, Mike."

"Don't be sorry. Sometimes the mundane can hide some peculiar things. There's still a thread left to pull. If Leo had anything to do with Erlich I have a Fed for a friend who just might come up with the answer." I snapped the lock shut on the trunk. "It just gives me a pain to have everything come up so damn hard."

"Really?" Her voice laughed.

I glanced up into the mirror on the dresser and felt that wild warmth steal into my stomach like an ebullient catalyst that pulled me taut as a bowstring and left my breath hanging in my throat.

"Something should be made easy for you then," she said.

Laura was standing there now, tall and lovely, the sun still with her in the rich loamy color of her skin, the nearly bleached white tone of her hair.

At her feet the bikini made a small puddle of black like a shadow, then she walked away from it to me and I was waiting for her.

CHAPTER 9

Night and the rain had come back to New York, the air musty with dust driven up by the sudden surge of the downpour. The bars were filled, the sheltered areas under marquees crowded and an empty taxi a rare treasure to be fought over.

But it was a night to think in. There is a peculiar anonymity you can enjoy in the city on a rainy night. You're alone, yet not alone. The other people around you are merely motion and sound and the sign of life whose presence averts the panic of being truly alone, yet who observe the rules of the city and stay withdrawn and far away when they are close.

How many times had Velda and I walked in the rain? She was big and our shoulders amost touched. We'd deliberately walk out of step so that our inside legs would touch rhythmically and if her arm wasn't tucked underneath mine we'd hold hands. There was a ring I had given her. I'd feel it under my fingers and she'd look at me and smile because she knew what that ring meant.

Where was she now? What had really happened? Little hammers would go at me when I thought of the days and hours since they had dragged me into Richie Cole's room to watch him die, but could it have been any other way?

Maybe not seven years ago. Not then. I wouldn't have had a booze-soaked head then. I would have had a gun and a ticket that could get me in and out of places and hands that could take care of anybody.

But now. Now I was an almost-nothing. Not quite, because I still had years of experience going for me and a reason to push. I was coming back little by little, but unless I stayed cute about it all I could be a pushover for any hardcase.

What I had to do now was think. I still had a small edge, but how long it would last was anybody's guess. So think, Mike, old soldier. Get your head going the way it's supposed to. You know who the key is. You've known it all along. Cole died with her name on his lips and ever since then she's been the key. But why? But why?

How could she still be alive?

Seven years is a long time to hide. Too long. Why? Why?

So think, old soldier. Go over the possibilities.

The rain came down a little harder and began to run off the brim of my hat. In a little while it seeped through the top of the cheap trench coat and I could feel the cold of it on my shoulders. And then I had the streets all alone again and the night and the city belonged only to me. I walked, so I was king. The others who huddled in the doorways and watched me with tired eyes were the lesser ones. Those who ran for the taxis were the scared ones. So I walked and I was able to think about Velda again. She had suddenly become *a case* and it had to be that way. It had to be cold and logical, otherwise it would vaporize into incredibility and there would be nothing left except to go back to where I had come from.

Think.

Who saw her die? No one. It was an assumption. Well assumed, but an assumption nevertheless.

Then, after seven years, who saw her alive? Richie Cole.

Sure, he had reason to know her. They were friends. War buddies. They had worked together. Once a year they'd meet for supper and a show and talk over old times. Hell, I'd done it myself with George and Earle, Ray, Mason and the others. It was nothing you could talk about to anybody else, though. Death and destruction you took part in could be shared only with those in range of the same enemy guns. With them you couldn't brag or lie. You simply recounted and wondered that you were still alive and renewed a friendship.

Cole couldn't have made a mistake. *He knew her.*

And Cole had been a pro. Velda was a pro. He had come looking for me because she had told him I was a pro and he had been disappointed at what he had seen. He had taken a look at me and his reason for staying alive died right then. Whatever it was, he didn't think I could do it. He saw a damned drunken bum who had lost every bit of himself years before and he died thinking she was going to die too and he was loathing me with eyes starting to film over with the nonexistence of death.

Richie Cole just didn't know me very well at all.

He had a chance to say the magic word and that made all the difference.

Velda.

Would it still be the same? How will *you* look after seven years? Hell, you should see me. You should see the way *I* look. And what's inside *you* after a time span like that? Things happen in seven years; things build, things dissolve. What happens to people in love? Seven years ago that's the way we were. In Love. Capital *L.* Had we stayed together time would only have lent maturity and quality to that which it served to improve.

But my love, my love, how could you look at me, me after seven years? You knew what I had been and called for me at last, but I wasn't what you expected at all. That big one you knew and loved is gone, kid, long gone, and you can't come back that big any more. Hell, Velda, you know that. You can't come back . . . you should have known what would happen to me. Damn, you knew me well enough. And it happened. So how can you yell for me now? *I know you knew what I'd be like, and you asked for me anyway.*

I let out a little laugh and only the rain could enjoy it with me. She knew, all right. You can't come back just as big. Either lesser or bigger. There was no other answer. She just didn't know the odds against the right choice.

There was a new man on the elevator now. I signed the night book, nodded to him and gave him my floor. I got off at eight and went down the hall, watching my shadow grow longer and longer from the single light behind me.

I had my keys in my hand, but I didn't need them at all. The door to 808 stood wide open invitingly, the lights inside throwing a warm glow over the dust and the furniture and when I closed it behind me I went through the anteroom to my office where Art Rickerby was sitting and picked up the sandwich and Blue Ribbon beer he had waiting for me and sat down on the edge of the couch and didn't say a word until I had finished both.

Art said, "Your friend Nat Drutman gave me the key."

"It's okay."

"I pushed him a little."

"He's been pushed before. If he couldn't read you right you wouldn't have gotten the key. Don't sell him short."

"I figured as much."

I got up, took off the soggy coat and hat and threw them across a chair. "What's with the visit? I hope you're not getting too impatient."

"No. Patience is something inbred. Nothing I can do will bring Richie back. All I can do is play the angles, the curves, float along the stream of time, then, my friend, something will bite, even on an unbaited hook."

"Shit."

"You know it's like that. You're a cop."

"A long time ago."

He watched me, a funny smile on his face. "No. *Now.* I know the signs. I've been in this business too long."

"So what do you want here?"

Rickerby's smile broadened. "I told you once. I'll do anything to get Richie's killer."

"Oh?"

He reached in his pocket and brought out an envelope. I took it from him, tore it open and read the folded card it contained on all four of its sides, then slid it into my wallet and tucked it away.

"Now I can carry a gun," I said.

"Legally. In any state."

"Thanks. What did you give up to get it?"

"Not a thing. Favors were owed me too. Our department is very—wise."

"They think it's smart to let me carry a rod again?"

"There aren't any complaints. You have your—ticket."

"It's a little different from the last one this state gave me."

"Don't look a gift horse in the mouth, my friend."

"Okay. Thanks."

"No trouble. I'm being smug."

"Why?"

He took off his glasses again, wiped them and put them back on. "Because I have found out all about you a person could find. You're going to do something I can't possibly do because you have the key to it all and won't let it go. Whatever your motives are, they aren't mine, but they encompass what I want and that's enough for me. Sooner or later you're going to name Richie's killer and that's all I want. In the meantime, rather than interfere with your operation, I'll do everything I can to supplement it. Do you understand?"

"I think so," I said.

"Good. Then I'll wait you out." He smiled, but there was nothing pleasant in his expression. "Some people are different from others. You're a killer, Mike. You've always been a killer. Somehow your actions have been justified and I think righteously so, but nevertheless, you're a killer. You're on a hunt again and I'm going to help you. There's just one thing I ask."

"What?"

"If you do find Richie's murderer before me, don't kill him."

I looked up from the fists I had made. "Why?"

"I want him, Mike. Let him be mine."

"What will you do with him?"

Rickerby's grin was damn near inhuman. It was a look I had seen before on other people and never would have expected from him. "A quick kill would be too good, Mike," he told me slowly. "But the law—this supposedly just, merciful provision—this is the most cruel of all. It lets you rot in a death cell for months and deteriorate slowly until you're only an accumulation of living cells with the consciousness of knowing you are about to die; then the creature is tied in a chair and jazzed with a hot shot that wipes him from the face of the earth with one big jolt and that's that."

"Pleasant thought," I said.

"Isn't it, though? Too many people think the sudden kill is the perfect answer for revenge. Ah, no, my friend. It's the waiting. It's the knowing beforehand that even the merciful provisions of a public trial will only result in what you already know—more waiting and further contemplation of that little room where you spend your last days with death in an oaken chair only a few yards away. And do you know what? I'll see that killer every day. I'll savor his anguish like a fine drink and be there as a witness when he burns and he'll see me and know why I'm there and when he's finished I'll be satisfied."

"You got a mean streak a yard wide, Rickerby."

"But it doesn't quite match yours, Mike."

"The hell it doesn't."

"No—you'll see what I mean some day. You'll see yourself express the violence of thought and action in a way I'd never do. True violence isn't in the deed itself. It's the contemplation and enjoyment of the deed."

"Come off it."

Rickerby smiled, the intensity of hatred he was filled with a moment ago seeping out slowly. If it had been me I would have been shaking like a leaf, but now he casually reached out for the can of beer, sipped at it coolly and put it down.

"I have some information you requested," he told me.

While I waited I walked behind the desk, sat down and pulled open the lower drawer. The shoulder holster was still supple although it had lain there seven years. I took off my jacket, slipped it on and put my coat back.

Art said, "I—managed to find out about Gerald Erlich."

I could feel the pulse in my arm throb against the arm of the chair. I still waited.

"Erlich is dead, my friend."

I let my breath out slowly, hoping my face didn't show how I felt.

"He died five years ago and his body was positively identified."

Five years ago! But he was supposed to have died during the war!

"He was found shot in the head in the Eastern Zone of Germany. After the war he had been fingerprinted and classified along with other prisoners of note so there was no doubt as to his identity." Art stopped a moment, studied me, then went on. "Apparently this man was trying to make the Western Zone. On his person were papers and articles that showed he had come out of Russia, there were signs that he had been under severe punishment and if you want to speculate, you might say that he had escaped from a prison and was tracked down just yards from freedom."

"That's pretty good information to come out of the Eastern Zone," I said.

Rickerby nodded sagely. "We have people there. They purposely investigate things of this sort. There's nothing coincidental about it."

"There's more."

His eyes were funny. They had an oblique quality as if they watched something totally foreign, something they had never realized could exist before. They watched and waited. Then he said, "Erlich had an importance we really didn't understand until lately. He was the nucleus of an

organization of espionage agents the like of which had
never been developed before and whose importance remained intact even after the downfall of the Third Reich.
It was an organization so ruthless that its members, in
order to pursue their own ends, would go with any government they thought capable of winning a present global
conflict and apparently they selected the Reds. To oppose
them and us meant fighting two battles, so it would be
better to support one until the other lost, then undermine
that one until it could take over."

"Crazy," I said.

"Is it?"

"They can't win."

"But they can certainly bring on some incredible devas-
tation."

"Then why kill Erlich?"

Art sat back and folded his hands together in a familiar
way. "Simple. He defected. He wanted out. Let's say he
got smart in his late years and realized the personal futility
of pushing this thing any further. He wanted to spend
a few years in peace."

It was reasonable in a way. I nodded.

"But he had to die," Art continued. "There was one
thing he knew that was known only to the next in line in
the chain of command, the ones taking over the organization."

"Like what?"

"He knew every agent in the group. He could bust the
whole shebang up if he spilled his guts to the West and
the idea of world conquest by the Reds or the others
would go smack down the drain."

"This you know?" I asked.

He shook his head. "No. Let's say I'm sure of it, but I
don't *know* it. At this point I really don't care. It's the
rest of the story I pulled out of the hat I'm interested in."
And now his eyes cocked themselves up at me again. "He
was tracked down and killed by one known to the Reds as
their chief assassin agent Gorlin, but to us as The Dragon."

If he could have had his hand on my chest, or even

have touched me anywhere he would have known what was happening. My guts would knot and churn and my head was filled with a wild flushing sensation of blood almost bursting through their walls. But he didn't touch me and he couldn't tell from my face so his eyes looked at me even a little more obliquely expecting even the slightest reaction and getting none. None at all.

"You're a cold-blooded bastard," he nearly whispered.

"You said that before."

He blinked owlishly behind his glasses and stood up, his coat over his arm. "You know where to reach me."

"I know."

"Do you need anything?"

"Not now. Thanks for the ticket."

"No trouble. Will you promise me something?"

"Sure."

"Just don't use that gun on The Dragon."

"I won't kill him, Art."

"No. Leave that for me. Don't spoil my pleasure or yours either."

He went out, closing the door softly behind him. I pulled the center desk drawer out, got the extra clip and the box of shells from the niche and closed the drawer.

The package I had mailed to myself was on the table by the door where Nat always put my packages when he had to take them from the mailman. I ripped it open, took out the .45, checked the action and dropped it in the holster.

Now it was just like old times.

I turned off the light in my office and went outside. I was reaching for the door when the phone on Velda's desk went off with a sudden jangling that shook me for a second before I could pick it up.

Her voice was rich and vibrant when she said hello and I wanted her right there with me right then. She knew it too, and her laugh rippled across the miles. She said, "Are you going to be busy tonight, Mike?"

Time was something I had too little of, but I had too little of her too. "Well—why?"

"Because I'm coming into your big city."

"Isn't it kind of late?"

"No. I have to be there at 10 P.M. to see a friend of yours and since I see no sense of wasting the evening I thought that whatever you have to do you can do it with me. Or can you?"

"It takes two to dance, baby."

She laughed again. "I didn't mean it *that* way."

"Sure, come on in. If I said not to I'd be lying. Who's my friend you have a date with?"

"An old friend and new enemy. Captain Chambers."

"What is this?"

"I don't know. He called and asked if I could come in. It would simplify things since his going out of his jurisdiction requires a lot of work."

"For Pete's sake—"

"Mike—I don't mind, really. If it has to do with Leo's death, well, I'll do anything. You know that."

"Yeah, but—"

"Besides, it gives me an excuse to see you even sooner than I hoped. Okay?"

"Okay."

"See you in a little while, Mike. Any special place?"

"Moriarty's at Sixth and Fifty-second. I'll be at the bar."

"Real quick," she said and hung up.

I held the disconnect bar down with my finger. Time. Seven years' worth just wasted and now there was none left. I let the bar up and dialed Hy Gardner's private number at the paper, hoping I'd be lucky enough to catch him in. I was.

He said, "Mike, if you're not doing anything, come on up here. I have to get my column out and I'll be done before you're here. I have something to show you."

"Important?"

"Brother, one word from you and everybody flips. Shake it up."

"Fifteen minutes."

"Good."

I hung up and pushed the phone back. When I did I

uncovered a heart scratched in the surface with something sharp. Inside it was a *V* and an *M. Velda and Mike.* I pulled the phone back to cover it, climbed into my coat and went outside. Just to be sure I still had the night to myself I walked down, out the back way through the drugstore then headed south on Broadway toward Hy's office.

Marilyn opened the door and hugged me hello, a pretty grin lighting her face up. She said, "Hy's inside waiting for you. He won't tell me what it's all about."

"You're his wife now, not his secretary anymore. You don't work for him."

"The heck I don't. But he still won't tell me."

"It's man talk, sugar."

"All right, I'll let you be. I'll get some coffee—and Mike—" I turned around.

"It's good to have you back."

When I winked she blew me a kiss and scurried out the door.

Hy was at his desk inside with his glasses up on his forehead, frowning at some sheets in his hand. They were covered with penciled notations apparently culled from another batch beside his elbow.

I pulled up a chair, sat down and let Hy finish what he was doing. Finally he glanced up, pulling his glasses down. "I got your message across."

"So?"

"So it was like I dropped a bomb in HQ. Over there they seem to know things we don't read in the paper here." He leaned forward and tapped the sheets in his hand. "This bit of The Dragon is the hottest item in the cold war, buddy. Are you sure you know what you're up to?"

"Uh-huh."

"Okay, I'll go along with you. The Reds are engaged in an operation under code name REN. It's a chase thing. Behind the Iron Curtain there has been a little hell to pay the last few years. Somebody was loose back there who could rock the whole Soviet system and that one had to be eliminated. That's where The Dragon came in. This one has been on that chase and was close to making his hit. Nobody knows what the score really is." He stopped then, pushed his glasses back up and said seriously, "or do they, Mike?"

"They?"

I should have been shaking. I should have been feeling some emotion, some wildness like I used to. What had happened? But maybe it was better this way. I could feel the weight of the .45 against my side and tightened my arm down on it lovingly. "They're after Velda," I said. "It's her. They're hunting her."

Hy squeezed his mouth shut and didn't say anything for a full minute. He laid the papers down and leaned back in his chair. "Why, Mike?"

"I don't know, Hy. I don't know why at all."

"If what I heard is true she doesn't have a chance."

"She has a chance," I told him softly.

"Maybe it really isn't her at all, Mike."

I didn't answer him. Behind us the door opened and Marilyn came in. She flipped an envelope on Hy's desk and set down the coffee container. "Here's a picture that just came off the wires. Del said you requested it."

Hy looked at me a little too quickly, opened the envelope and took out the photo. He studied it, then passed it across.

It really wasn't a good picture at all. The original had been fuzzy to start with and transmission electrically hadn't improved it any. She stood outside a building, a tall girl with seemingly black hair longer than I remembered it, features not quite clear and whose shape and posture were hidden under bulky Eastern European style clothing. Still, there was that indefinable something, some subtlety in the way she stood, some trait that came through the clothing and poor photography that I couldn't help but see.

I handed the photo back. "It's Velda."

"My German friend said the picture was several years old."

"Who had it?"

"A Red agent who was killed in a skirmish with some West German cops. It came off his body. I'd say he had been assigned to REN too and the picture was for identification purposes."

"Is this common information?"

Hy shook his head. "I'd say no. Rather than classify this thing government sources simply refuse to admit it exists. We came on it separately."

I said, "The government knows it exists."

"You know too damn much, Mike."

"No, not enough. I don't know where she is now."

"I can tell you one thing," Hy said.

"Oh?"

"She isn't in Europe any longer. The locale of REN has changed. The Dragon has left Europe. His victim got away somehow and all indications point to them both being in this country."

Very slowly, I got up, put my coat and hat on and stretched the dampness out of my shoulders. I said, "Thanks, Hy."

"Don't you want your coffee?"

"Not now."

He opened a drawer, took out a thick Manila envelope and handed it to me. "Here. You might want to read up a little more on Senator Knapp. It's confidential stuff. Gives you an idea of how big he was. Save it for me."

"Sure." I stuck it carelessly in my coat pocket. "Thanks."

Marilyn said, "You all right, Mike?"

I grinned at her a little crookedly. "I'm okay."

"You don't look right," she insisted.

Hy said, "Mike—"

And I cut him short. "I'll see you later, Hy." I grinned at him too. "And thanks. Don't worry about me." I patted the gun under my coat. "I have a friend along now. Legally."

While I waited, I read about just how great a guy Leo

Knapp had been. His career had been cut short at a tragic spot because it was evident that in a few more years he would have been the big man on the political scene. It was very evident that here had been one of the true powers behind the throne, a man initially responsible for military progress and missile production in spite of opposition from the knotheaded liberals and "better-Red-than-dead" slobs. He had thwarted every attack and forced through the necessary programs and in his hands had been secrets of vital importance that made him a number one man in the Washington setup. His death came at a good time for the enemy. The bullet that killed him came from the gun of The Dragon. A bullet from the same gun killed Richie Cole and almost killed me twice. A bullet from that same gun was waiting to kill Velda.

She came in then, the night air still on her, shaking the rain from her hair, laughing when she saw me. Her hand was cool when she took mine and climbed on the stool next to me. John brought her a Martini and me another Blue Ribbon. We raised the glasses in a toast and drank the top off them.

"Good to see you," I said.

"You'll never know," she smiled.

"Where are you meeting Pat?"

She frowned, then, "Oh, Captain Chambers. Why, right here." She glanced at her watch. "In five minutes. Shall we sit at a table?"

"Let's." I picked up her glass and angled us across the room to the far wall. "Does Pat know I'll be here?"

"I didn't mention it."

"Great. Just great."

Pat was punctual, as usual. He saw me but didn't change expression. When he said hello to Laura he sat beside her and only then looked at me. "I'm glad you're here too."

"That's nice."

He was a mean, cold cop if ever there was one, his face a mask you couldn't penetrate until you looked into his eyes and saw the hate and determination there. "Where do you find your connections, Mike?"

"Why?"

"It's peculiar how a busted private dick, a damn drunken pig in trouble up to his ears can get a gun-carrying privilege we can't break. How do you do it, punk?"

I shrugged, not feeling like arguing with him. Laura looked at the two of us, wondering what was going on.

"Well, you might need it at that if you keep getting shot at. By the way, I got a description of your back alley friend. He was seen by a rather observant kid in the full light of the street lamp. Big guy, about six-two with dark curly hair and a face with deep lines in the cheeks. His cheekbones were kind of high so he had kind of an Indian look. Ever see anybody like that?"

He was pushing me now, doing anything to set me off so he'd have a reason to get at me but sure, I saw a guy like that. He drove past me on the Thruway and I thought he was a tired driver, then he shot at me later and now I know damn well who he is. You call him The Dragon. He had a face I'd see again someday, a face I couldn't miss.

I said, "No, I don't know him." It wasn't quite a lie.

Pat smiled sardonically, "I have a feeling you will."

"So okay, I'll try to catch up with him for you."

"You do that, punk. Meanwhile I'll catch up with you. I'm putting you into this thing tighter than ever."

"Me?"

"That's right. That's why I'm glad you're here. It saves seeing you later." He had me curious now and knew it, and he was going to pull it out all the way. "There is a strange common denominator running throughout our little murder puzzle here. I'm trying to find out just what it all means."

"Please go on," Laura said.

"Gems. For some reason I can't get them out of my mind. Three times they cross in front of me." He looked at me, his eyes narrowed, "The first time when my old friend here let a girl die because of them, then when

Senator Knapp was killed a batch of paste jewels were taken from the safe, and later a man known for his gem smuggling was killed with the same gun. It's a recurrent theme, isn't it, Mike? You're supposed to know about these things. In fact, it must have occurred to you too. You were quick enough about getting upstate to see Mrs. Knapp here."

"Listen, Pat."

"Shut up. There's more." He reached in his pocket and tugged at a cloth sack. "We're back to the gems again." He pulled the top open, spilled the sack upside down and watched the flood of rings, brooches and bracelets make a sparkling mound of brilliance on the table between us.

"Paste, pure paste, Mrs. Knapp, but I think they are yours."

Her hand was shaking when she reached out to touch them. She picked up the pieces one by one, examining them, then shaking her head. "Yes—they're mine! But where—"

"A pathetic old junkman was trying to peddle them in a pawnshop. The broker called the cops and we grabbed the guy. He said he found them in a garbage can a long time ago and kept them until now to sell. He figured they were stolen, all right, but didn't figure he'd get picked up like he did."

"Make your connection, Pat. So far all you showed was that a smart crook recognized paste jewelry and dumped it."

His eyes had a vicious cast to them this time. "I'm just wondering about the original gem robbery, the one your agency was hired to prevent. The name was Mr. and Mrs. Rudolph Civac. I'm wondering what kind of a deal was really pulled off there. You sent in Velda but wouldn't go yourself. I'm thinking that maybe you turned sour away back there and tried for a big score and fouled yourself up in it somehow."

His hands weren't showing so I knew one was sitting on a gun butt. I could feel myself going around the edges but hung on anyway. "You're nuts," I said, "I never even saw Civac. He made the protection deal by phone. I never laid eyes on him."

Pat felt inside his jacket and came out with a four-by-five glossy photo. "Well take a look at what your deceased customer looked like. I've been backtracking all over that case, even as cold as it is. Something's going to come up on it, buddy boy, and I hope you're square in the middle of it." He forgot me for a moment and turned to Laura. "Do you postively identify these, Mrs. Knapp?"

"Oh, yes. There's an accurate description of each piece on file and on the metal there's—"

"I saw the hallmarks."

"This ring was broken—see here where this prong is off—yes, these are mine."

"Fine. You can pick them up at my office tomorrow if you want to. I'll have to hold them until then though."

"That's all right."

He snatched the picture out of my fingers and put it back in his pocket. "You I'll be seeing soon," he told me.

I didn't answer him. I nodded, but that was all. He looked at me a moment, scowled, went to say something and changed his mind. He told Laura goodbye and walked to the door.

Fresh drinks came and I finished mine absently. Laura chuckled once and I glanced up. "You've been quiet a long time. Aren't we going to do the town?"

"Do you mind if we don't?"

She raised her eyebrows, surprised, but not at all unhappy. "No, do you want to do something else?"

"Yes. Think."

"Your place?" she asked mischievously.

"I don't have a place except my office."

"We've been there before," she teased.

But I had kissed Velda there too many times before too. "No," I said.

Laura leaned forward, serious now. "It's important, isn't it?"

"Yes."

"Then let's get out of the city entirely. Let's go back

upstate to where it's cool and quiet and you can think right. Would you like to do that?"

"All right."

I paid the bill and we went outside to the night and the rain to flag down a cab to get us to the parking lot. She had to do it for me because the only thing I could think of was the face in that picture Pat had showed me.

Rudolph Civac was the same as Gerald Erlich.

CHAPTER 10

I couldn't remember the trip at all. I was asleep before we reached the West Side Drive and awakened only when she shook me. Her voice kept calling to me out of a fog and for a few seconds I thought it was Velda, then I opened my eyes and Laura was smiling at me. "We're home, Mike."

The rain had stopped, but in the stillness of the night I could hear the soft dripping from the shadows of the blue spruces around the house. Beyond them a porch and inside light threw out a pale yellow glow. "Won't your servants have something to say about me coming in?"

"No, I'm alone at night. The couple working for me come only during the day."

"I haven't seen them yet."

"Each time you were here they had the day off."

I made an annoyed grimace. "You're nuts, kid. You should keep somebody around all the time after what happened."

Her hand reached out and she traced a line around my mouth. "I'm trying to," she said. Then she leaned over and brushed me with lips that were gently damp and sweetly warm, the tip of her tongue a swift dart of flame, doing it too quickly for me to grab her to make it last.

"Quit brainwashing me," I said.

She laughed at me deep in her throat. "Never, Mister Man. I've been too long without you."

Rather than hear me answer she opened the door and slid out of the car. I came around from the other side and we went up the steps into the house together. It was a funny feeling, this coming home sensation. There was the house and the woman and the mutual desire, an instinctive demanding passion we shared, one for the other, yet realizing that there were other things that came first and not caring because there was always later.

There was a huge couch in the living room of soft, aged leather, a hidden hi-fi that played Dvorak, Beethoven and Tchaikovsky and somewhere in between Laura had gotten into yards of flowing nylon that did nothing to hide the warmth of her body or restrain the luscious bloom of her thighs and breasts. She lay there in my arms quietly, giving me all of the moment to enjoy as I pleased, only her sometimes-quickened breathing indicating her pleasure as I touched her lightly, caressing her with my fingertips. Her eyes were closed, a small satisfied smile touched the corners of her mouth and she snuggled into me with a sigh of contentment.

How long I sat there and thought about it I couldn't tell. I let it drift through my mind from beginning to end, the part I knew and the part I didn't know. Like always, a pattern was there. You can't have murder without a pattern. It weaves in and out, fabricating an artful tapestry, and while the background colors were apparent from the beginning it is only at the last that the picture itself emerges. But who was the weaver? Who sat invisibly behind the loom with shuttles of death in one hand and skeins of lives in the other? I fell asleep trying to peer behind the gigantic framework of that murder factory, a sleep so deep, after so long, that there was nothing I thought about or remembered afterward.

I was alone when the bright shaft of sunlight pouring in the room awakened me. I was stretched out comfortably, my shoes off, my tie loose and a light Indian blanket over me. I threw it off, put my shoes back on and stood up. It took me a while to figure out what was wrong, then I saw the .45 in the shoulder holster draped over the back of a chair with my coat over it and while I was reaching for it she came in with all the exuberance of a summer morning, a tray of coffee in her hands and blew me a kiss.

"Well hello," I said.

She put the tray down and poured the coffee. "You were hard to undress."

"Why bother?"

Laura looked up laughing. "It's not easy to sleep with a man wearing a gun." She held out a cup. "Here, have some coffee. Sugar and milk?"

"Both. And I'm glad it's milk and not cream."

She fixed my cup, stirring it too. "You're a snob, Mike. In your own way you're a snob." She made a face at me and grinned. "But I love snobs."

"You should be used to them. You travel in classy company."

"They aren't snobs like you. They're just scared people putting on a front. You're the real snob. Now kiss me good morning—or afternoon. It's one o'clock." She reached up offering her mouth and I took it briefly, but even that quick touch bringing back the desire again.

Laura slid her hand under my arm and walked me through the house to the porch and out to the lawn by the pool. The sun overhead was brilliant and hot, the air filled with the smell of the mountains. She said, "Can I get you something to eat?"

I tightened my arm on her hand. "You're enough for right now."

She nuzzled my shoulder, wrinkled her nose and grinned. We both pulled out aluminum and plastic chairs, and while she went inside for the coffeepot I settled down in mine.

Now maybe I could think.

She poured another cup, knowing what was going through my mind. When she sat down opposite me she said, "Mike, would it be any good to tell me about it?

I'm a good listener. I'll be somebody you can aim hypothetical questions at. Leo did this with me constantly. He called me his sounding board. He could think out loud, but doing it alone he sounded foolish to himself so he'd do it with me." She paused, her eyes earnest, wanting to help. "I'm yours for anything if you want me, Mike."

"Thanks, kitten."

I finished the coffee and put the cup down.

"You're afraid of something," she said.

"Not of. *For*. Like for you, girl. I told you once I was a trouble character. Wherever I am there's trouble and when you play guns there are stray shots and I don't want you in the way of any."

"I've already been there, remember?"

"Only because I wasn't on my toes. I've slowed up. I've been away too damn long and I'm not careful."

"Are you careful now?"

My eyes reached hers across the few feet that separated us. "No. I'm being a damn fool again. I doubt if we were tailed here, but it's only a doubt. I have a gun in the house, but we could be dead before I reached it."

She shrugged unconcernedly. "There's the shotgun in the bathhouse."

"That's still no good. It's a pro game. There won't be any more second chances. You couldn't reach the shotgun either. It's around the pool and in the dark."

"So tell me about it, Mike. Think to me and maybe it will end even faster and we can have ourselves to ourselves. If you want to think, or be mad or need a reaction, think to me."

I said, "Don't you like living?"

A shadow passed across her face and the knuckles of her hand on the arms of the chair went white. "I stopped living when Leo died. I thought I'd never live again."

"Kid—"

"No, it's true, Mike. I know all the objections you can put up about our backgrounds and present situations but it still doesn't make any difference. It doesn't alter a simple fact that I knew days ago. I fell in love with you, Mike. I took one look at you and fell in love, knowing then that objections would come, troubles would be a heritage and you might not love me at all."

"Laura—"

"Mike—I started to live again. I thought I was dead and I started to live again. Have I pushed you into anything?"

"No."

"And I won't. You can't push a man. All you can do is try, but you just can't push a man and a woman should know that. It she can, then she doesn't have a man."

She waved me to be quiet and went on. "I don't care how you feel toward me. I hope, but that is all. I'm quite content knowing I can live again and no matter where you are you'll know that I love you. It's a peculiar kind of courtship, but these are peculiar times and I don't care if it has to be like this. Just be sure of one thing. You can have anything you want from me, Mike. Anything. There's nothing you can ask me to do that I won't do. Not one thing. That's how completely yours I am. There's a way to be sure. Just ask me. But I won't push you. If you ask me never to speak of it again, then I'll do that too. You see, Mike, it's a sort of hopeless love, but I'm living again, I'm loving, and you can't stop me from loving you. It's the only exception to what you can ask—I won't stop loving you.

"But to answer your question, yes, I like living. You brought me alive. I was dead before."

There was a beauty about her then that was indescribable. I said, "Anything you know can be too much. You're a target now. I don't want you to be an even bigger one."

"I'll only die if you die," she said simply.

"Laura—"

She wouldn't let me finish. "Mike—do you love me—at all?"

The sun was a honeyed cloud in her hair, bouncing off the deep brown of her skin to bring out the classic loveliness of her features. She was so beautifully deep-breasted, her stomach molding itself hollow beneath the outline of her ribs, the taut fabric of the sleeveless playsuit accentuating the timeless quality that was Laura.

I said, "I think so, Laura. I don't know for sure. It's just that I—can't tell anymore."

"It's enough for now," she said. "That little bit will grow because it has to. You were in love before, weren't you?"

I thought of Charlotte and Velda and each was like being suddenly shot low down when knowledge precedes breathlessness and you know it will be a few seconds before the real pain hits.

"Yes," I told her.

"Was it the same?"

"It's never the same. You are—different."

She nodded. "I know, Mike. I know." She waited, then added, "It will be—the other one—or me, won't it?"

There was no sense lying to her. "That's right."

"Very well. I'm satisfied. So now do you want to talk to me? Shall I listen for you?"

I leaned back in the chair, let my face look at the sun with my eyes closed and tried to start at the beginning. Not the beginning the way it happened, but the beginning the way I thought it could have happened. It was quite a story. Now I had to see if it made sense.

I said:

"There are only principals in this case. They are odd persons, and out of it entirely are the police and the Washington agencies. The departments only know results, not causes, and although they suspect certain things they are not in a position to be sure of what they do. We eliminate them and get to basic things. They may be speculative, but they are basic and lead to conclusions.

"The story starts at the end of World War I with an espionage team headed by Gerald Erlich who, with others, had visions of a world empire. Oh, it wasn't a new dream. Before him there had been Alexander and Caesar and Napoleon so he was only picking up an established trend. So Erlich's prime mover was nullified and he took on another—Hitler. Under that regime he became great and his organization became more nearly perfected, and when Hitler died and the Third Reich became extinct this was nothing too, for now the world was more truly divided. Only two parts remained, the East and the West and he chose, for the moment, to side with the East. Gerald Erlich picked the Red Government as his next prime mover. He thought they would be the ultimate victors in the conquest of the world, then, when the time was right, he would take over from them.

"Ah, but how time and circumstances can change. He didn't know that the Commies were equal to him in *their* dreams of world empire. He didn't realize that they would find *him* out and use *him* while he thought they were in *his* hands. They took over his organization. Like they did the rest of the world they control, they took his corrupt group and corrupted it even further. But an organization they could control. The leader of the organization, a fanatical one, they knew they couldn't. He had to go. Like dead.

"However, Erlich wasn't quite that stupid. He saw the signs and read them right. He wasn't young any longer and his organization had been taken over. His personal visions of world conquest didn't seem quite so important any-more and the most important thing was to stay alive as best he could and the place to do it was in the States. So he came here. He married well under the assumed name of Rudy Civac to a rich widow and all was well in his private world for a time.

"Then, one day, they found him. His identity was revealed. He scrambled for cover. It was impossible to ask for police protection so he did the next best thing, he called a private detective agency and as a subterfuge, used his wife's jewels as the reason for needing security. Actually, he wanted guns around. He wanted shooting protection.

"Now here the long arm of fate struck a second time. Not coincidence—but fate, pure unblemished fate. I sent Velda. During the war she had been young, beautiful, intelligent, a perfect agent to use against men. She was in the O.S.S., the O.S.I. and another highly secretive group and assigned to Operation Butterfly Two which was nailing Gerald Erlich and breaking down his organization. The war ended before it could happen, she was discharged, came with me into the agency because it was a work she knew and we stayed together until Rudy Civac called for protection. He expected me. He got her.

"Fate struck for sure when she saw him. She knew who he was. She knew that a man like that had to be stopped because he might still have his purposes going for him. There was the one thing she knew that made Gerald Elrich the most important man in the world right then. He knew the names and identities of every major agent he ever had working for him and these were such dedicated people they never stopped working—and now they were working for the Reds.

"Coincidence here. Or Fate. Either will do. This was the night the Red agents chose to act. They hit under the guise of burglars. They abducted Rudy Civac, his wife and Velda. They killed the wife, but they needed Rudy to find out exactly what he knew.

"And Velda played it smart. She made like she was part of Civac's group just to stay alive and it was conceivable that she had things they must know too. This we can't forget—Velda was a trained operative—she had prior experience even I didn't know about. Whatever she did she made it stick. They got Civac and her back into Europe and into Red territory and left the dead wife and the stolen jewels as a red herring that worked like a charm, and while Velda was in the goddamn Russian country I was drinking myself into a lousy pothole—"

She spoke for the first time. She said, "Mike—" and I squeezed open my eyes and looked at her.

"Thanks."

"It's all right. I understand."

I closed my eyes again and let the picture form.

"The Commies aren't the greatest brains in the world, though. Those stupid peasants forgot one thing. Both Civac—or Erlich—and Velda were pros. Someplace along the line they slipped and both of them cut out. They got loose inside the deep Iron Curtain and from then on the chase was on.

"Brother, I bet heads rolled after that. Anyway, when they knew two real hotshots were on the run they called in the top man to make the chase. *The Dragon.* Comrade Gorlin. But I like The Dragon better. I'll feel more like St. George when I kill him. *And won't Art hate me for that, I thought.*

"The chase took seven years. I think I know what happened during that time. Civac and Velda had to stay together to pool their escape resources. One way or another Velda was able to get things from Civac—or Erlich—and the big thing was those names. I'll bet she made him recount every one and she committed them to memory and carried them in her head all the way through so that she was fully as important now as Civac was.

"Don't underplay the Reds. They're filthy bastards, every one, but they're on the ball when it comes to thinking out the dirty work. They're so used to playing it themselves that it's second nature to them. Hell, they knew what happened. They knew Velda was as big as Erlich now—perhaps even bigger. Erlich's dreams were on the decline . . . what Velda knew would put us on the upswing again, so above all, she had to go.

"So The Dragon in his chase concentrated on those two. Eventually he caught up with Erlich and shot him. That left Velda. Now he ran into a problem. During her war years she made a lot of contacts. One of them was Richie Cole. They'd meet occasionally when he was off assignment and talk over the old days and stayed good friends. She knew he was in Europe and somehow or other made contact with him. There wasn't time enough to pass on what she had memorized and it wasn't safe to write it down, so the answer was to get Velda back to the States with her information. There wasn't even time to assign the job to a proper agency.

"Richie Cole broke orders and took it upon himself to protect Velda and came back to the States. He knew he was followed. He knew The Dragon would make him a target—he knew damn well there wouldn't be enough time to do the right thing, but Velda had given him a name. She gave him me and a contact to make with an old newsie we both knew well.

"Sure, Cole tried to make the contact, but The Dragon shot him first. Trouble was, Cole didn't die. He told off until they got hold of me because Velda told him I was so damn big I could break the moon apart in my bare hands and he figured if she said it I really could. Then he saw me."

I put my face in my hands to rub out the picture. *"Then he saw me!"*

"Mike—"

"Let's face it, kid. I was a drunk."

"Mike—"

"Shut up. Let me talk."

Laura didn't answer, but her eyes hoped I wasn't going off the deep end, so I stopped a minute, poured some coffee, drank it, then started again.

"Once again those goddamn Reds were smart. They backtracked Velda and found out about me. They knew what Richie Cole was trying to do. Richie knew where Velda was and wanted to tell me. He died before he did. They thought he left the information with Old Dewey and killed the old man. They really thought I knew and they put a tail on me to see if I made a contact. They tore Dewey's place and my place apart looking for information they thought Cole might have passed to me. Hell, The Dragon even tried to kill me because he thought I wasn't really important at all and was better out of the way."

I leaned back in the chair, my insides feeling hollow all of a sudden. Laura asked, "Mike, what's the matter?"

"Something's missing. Something big."

"Please don't talk any more."

"It's not that. I'm just tired, I guess. It's hard to come back to normal this fast."

"If we took a swim it might help."

I opened my eyes and looked at her and grinned. "Sick of hearing hard luck stories?"

"No."

"Any questions?"

She nodded. "Leo. Who shot him?"

I said, "In this business guns can be found anywhere. I'm never surprised to see guns with the same ballistics used in different kills. Did you know the same gun that shot your husband and Richie Cole was used in some small kill out West?"

"No, I didn't know that."

"There seemed to be a connection through the jewels. Richie's cover was that of a sailor and smuggler. Your jewels were missing. Pat made that a common factor. I don't believe it."

"Could Leo's position in government—well, as you intimated—"

"There is a friend of mine who says no. He has reason to know the facts. I'll stick with him."

"Then Leo's death is no part of what you are looking for?"

"I don't think so. In a way I'm sorry. I wish I could help avenge him too. He was a great man."

"Yes, he was."

"I'll take you up on that swim."

"The suits are in the bathhouse."

"That should be fun," I said.

In the dim light that came through the ivy-screened windows we turned our backs and took off our clothes. When you do that deliberately with a woman, it's hard to talk and you are conscious only of the strange warmth and the brief, fiery contact when skin meets skin and a crazy desire to turn around and watch or to grab and hold or do anything except what you said you'd do when the modest moment was in reality a joke—but you didn't quite want it to be a joke at all.

Then before we could turn it into something else and while we could still treat it as a joke, we had the bathing suits on and she grinned as she passed by me. I reached for

her, stopped her, then turned because I saw something
else that left me cold for little *ticks* of time.

Laura said, "What is it, Mike?"

I picked the shotgun out of the corner of the room. The
building had been laid up on an extension of the tennis
court outside and the temporary floor was clay. Where the
gun rested by the door water from the outside shower had
seeped in and wet it down until it was a semi-firm sub-
stance, a blue putty you could mold in your hand.

*She had put the shotgun down muzzle first and both
barrels were plugged with clay and when I picked it up it
was like somebody had taken a bite out of the blue glop
with a cookie cutter two inches deep!*

Before I opened it I asked her, "Loaded?"

"Yes."

I thumbed the lever and broke the gun. It fell open and
I picked out the two twelve-guage Double O shells, then
slapped the barrels against my palm until the cores of clay
emerged far enough for me to pull them out like the deadly
plugs they were.

She saw the look on my face and frowned, not knowing
what to say. So I said it instead. "Who put the gun here?"

"I did."

"I thought you knew how to handle it?" There was a
rasp in my voice you could cut with a knife.

"Leo—showed me how to shoot it."

"He didn't show you how to handle it, apparently."

"Mike—"

"Listen, Laura, and you listen good. You play with guns
and you damn well better *know* how to handle them. You
went and stuck this baby's nose down in the muck and do
you know what would happen if you ever tried to shoot it?"

Her eyes were frightened at what she saw in my face and
she shook her head. "Well, damn it, you listen then. Without even thinking you stuck this gun in heavy clay and
plugged both barrels. It's loaded with high-grade sporting
ammunition of the best quality and if you ever pulled the
trigger you would have had one infinitesimal span of life
between the big then and the big now because when you

did the back blast in that gun would have wiped you right off the face of the earth."

"Mike—"

"No—keep quiet and listen. It'll do you good. You won't make the mistake again. That barrel would unpeel like a tangerine and you'd get that whole charge right down your lovely throat and if ever you want to give a police medical examiner a job to gag a maggot, that's the way to do it. They'd have to go in and scrape your brains up with a silent butler and pick pieces of your skull out of the woodwork with needle-nosed pliers. I saw eyeballs stuck to a wall one time and if you want to *really* see a disgusting sight, try that. They're bigger than you would expect them to be and they leak fluid all the time they look at you trying to lift them off the boards and then you have no place to put them except in your hand and drop them in the bucket with the rest of the pieces. They float on top and keep watching you until you put on the lid."

"*Mike!*"

"Damn it, shut up! Don't play guns stupidly around me! You did it, now listen!"

Both hands covered her mouth and she was almost ready to vomit.

"The worst of all is the neck because the head is gone and the neck spurts blood for a little bit while the heart doesn't know its vital nerve center is gone—and do you know how high the blood can squirt? No? Then let me tell you. It doesn't just ooze. It goes up under pressure for a couple of feet and covers everything in the area and you wouldn't believe just how much blood the body has in it until you see a person suddenly become headless and watch what happens. I've been there. I've had it happen. *Don't let it happen to you!*"

She let her coffee go on the other side of the door and I didn't give a damn because anybody that careless with a shotgun or any other kind of a gun needs it like that to make them remember. I wiped the barrels clean, reloaded the gun and put it down in place, butt first.

When I came out Laura said, "Man, are you mean."

"It's not a new saying." I still wasn't over my mad.

Her smile was a little cockeyed, but a smile nevertheless. "Mike—I understand. Please?"

"Really?"

"Yes."

"Then you watch it. I play guns too much. It's my business. I hate to see them abused."

"Please, Mike?"

"Okay. I made my point."

"Nobly, to say the least. I usually have a strong stomach."

"Go have some coffee."

"Oh, Mike."

"So take a swim," I told her and grinned. It was the way I felt and the grin was the best I could do. She took a run and a dive and hit the water, came up stroking for the other side, then draped her arms on the edge of the drain and waited for me.

I went in slowly, walking up to the edge, then I dove in and stayed on the bottom until I got to the other side. The water made her legs fuzzy, distorting them to Amazonian proportions, enlarging the cleft and swells and declavities of her belly, then I came up to where all was real and shoved myself to concrete surface and reached down for Laura.

She said, "Better?" when I pulled her to the top.

I was looking past her absently. "Yes. I just remembered something."

"Not about the gun, Mike."

"No, not about the gun."

"Should I know?"

"It doesn't matter. I don't really know myself yet. It's just a point."

"Your eyes look terribly funny."

"I know."

"Mike—"

"What?"

"Can I help?"

"No."

"You're going to leave me now, aren't you?"

"Yes, I am."

"Will you come back?"

I couldn't answer her.

"It's between the two of us, isn't it?"

"The girl hunters are out," I said.

"But will you come back?"

My mind was far away, exploring the missing point. "Yes," I said, "I have to come back."

"You loved her."

"I did."

"Do you love me at all?"

I turned around and looked at this woman. She was mine now, beautiful, wise, the way a woman should be formed for a man like I was, lovely, always naked in my sight, always incredibly blonde and incredibly tanned, the difference in color—or was it comparison—a shocking, sensual thing. I said, "I love you, Laura. Can I be mistaken?"

She said, "No, you can't be mistaken."

"I have to find her first. She's being hunted. Everybody is hunting her. I loved her a long time ago so I owe her that much. She asked for me."

"Find her, Mike."

I nodded. I had the other key now. "I'll find her. She's the most important thing in this old world today. What she knows will decide the fate of nations. Yes, I'll find her."

"Then will you come back?"

"Then I'll come back," I said.

Her arms reached out and encircled me, her hands holding my head, her fingers tight in my hair. I could feel every inch of her body pressed hard against mine, forcing itself to meet me, refusing to give at all.

"I'm going to fight her for you," she said.

"Why?"

"Because you're mine now."

"Girl," I said, "I'm no damn good to anybody. Look good and you'll see a corn ear husked, you know?"

"I know. So I eat husks."

"Damn it, don't fool around!"

"Mike!"

"Laura—"

"You say it nice, Mike—but there's something in your voice that's terrible and I can sense it. If you find her, what will you do?"

"I can't tell."

"Will you still come back?"

"Damn it, I don't know."

"Why don't you know, Mike?"

I looked down at her. "Because I don't know what I'm really like any more. Look—do you know what I *was?* Do you know that a judge and jury took me down and the whole world once ripped me to little bits? It was only Velda who stayed with me then."

"That was then. How long ago was it?"

"Nine years maybe."

"Were you married?"

"No."

"Then I can claim part of you. I've had part of you." She let go of me and stood back, her eyes calm as they looked into mine. "Find her, Mike. Make your decision. Find her and take her. Have you ever had her at all?"

"No."

"You've had *me.* Maybe you're more mine than hers."

"Maybe."

"Then find her." She stepped back, her hands at her side. "If what you said was true then she deserves this much. You find her, Mike. I'm willing to fight you for anybody—but not somebody you think is dead. Not somebody you think you owe a debt to. Let me love you my own way. It's enough for me at least. Do you understand that?"

For a while we stood there. I looked at her. I looked away. I said, "Yes, I understand."

"Come back when you've decided."

"You have all of Washington to entertain."

Laura shook her head. Her hair was a golden swirl and

she said, "The hell with Washington. I'll be waiting for you."

Velda, Laura. The names were so similar. Which one? After seven years of nothingness, which one? Knowing what I did, which one? Yesterday was then. Today was now. Which one?

I said, "All right, Laura, I'll find out, then I'll come back."

"Take my car."

"Thanks."

And now I had to take her. My fingers grabbed her arms and pulled her close to where I could kiss her and taste the inside of her mouth and feel the sensuous writhing of her tongue against mine because this was the woman I knew I was coming back to.

The *Girl Hunters*. We all wanted the same one and for reasons of a long time ago. We would complete the hunt, but what would we do with the kill?

She said, "After that you shouldn't leave."

"I have to," I said.

"Why?"

"She had to get in this country someway. I think I know how."

"You'll find her then come back?"

"Yes," I said, and let my hands roam over her body so that she knew there could never be anybody else, and when I was done I held her off and made her stay there while I went inside to put on the gun and the coat and go back to the new Babylon that was the city.

CHAPTER 11

And once again it was night, the city coming into its nether life like a minion of Count Dracula. The bright light of day that could strip away the facade of sham and lay bare the coating of dirt was gone now, and to the onlooker the unreal became real, the dirt had changed into subtle colors under artificial lights and it was as if all of that vast pile of concrete and steel and glass had been built only to live at night.

I left the car at the Sportsmen's Parking Lot on the corner of Eighth and Fifty-second, called Hy Gardner and told him to meet me at the Blue Ribbon on Forty-fourth, then started my walk to the restaurant thinking of the little things I should have thought of earlier.

The whole thing didn't seem possible, all those years trapped in Europe. You could walk around the world half a dozen times in seven years. But you wouldn't be trapped then. The thing was, they *were* trapped. Had Velda or Erlich been amateurs they would have been captured without much trouble, but being pros they edged out. Almost. That made Velda even better than he had been.

Somehow, it didn't seem possible.

But it was.

Hy had reached the Blue Ribbon before me and waited

at a table sipping a stein of rich, dark beer. I nodded at the waiter and he went back for mine. We ordered, ate, and only then did Hy bother to give me his funny look over the cigar he lit up. "It's over?"

"It won't be long now."

"Do we talk about it here?"

"Here's as good as any. It's more than you can put in your column."

"You let me worry about space."

So he sat back and let me tell him what I had told Laura, making occasional notes, because now was the time to make notes. I told him what I knew and what I thought and where everybody stood, and every minute or so he'd glance up from his sheets with an expression of pure incredulity, shake his head and write some more. When the implications of the total picture began really to penetrate, his teeth clamped down on the cigar until it was half hanging out of his mouth unlit, then he threw it down on his plate and put a fresh one in its place.

When I finished he said, "Mike—do you realize what you have hold of?"

"I know."

"How can you stay so damn calm?"

"Because the rough part has just started."

"Ye gods, man—"

"You know what's missing, don't you?"

"Sure. You're missing something in the head. You're trying to stand off a whole political scheme that comes at you with every force imaginable no matter where you are. Mike, you don't fight these guys alone!"

"Nuts. It looks like I have to. I'm not exactly an accredited type character. Who would listen to me?"

"Couldn't this Art Rickerby—"

"He has one purpose in mind. He wants whoever killed Richie Cole."

"That doesn't seem likely. He's a trained Federal agent."

"So what? When something hits you personally, patriotism can go by the boards awhile. There are plenty of other agents. He wants a killer and knows I'll eventually come

up with him. Like Velda's a key to one thing, I'm a key
to another. They think that I'm going to stumble over
whatever it was Richie Cole left for me. I know what it
was now. So do you, don't you?"

"Yes," Hy said. "It was Velda's location, wherever she
is."

"That's right. They don't know if I know or if I'll find
out. You can damn well bet that they know he stayed alive
waiting for me to show. They can't even be sure if he just
clued me. They can't be sure of anything, but they know
that I have to stay alive if they want to find Velda too."

Hy's eyes went deep in thought. "Alive? They tried to
shoot you twice, didn't they?"

"Fine, but neither shot connected and I can't see a top
assassin missing a shot. Both times I was a perfect target."

"Why the attempt then?"

"I'll tell you why," I said. I leaned on the table feeling
my hands go open and shut wanting to squeeze the life out
of somebody. "Both tries were deliberately sour. They
were pushing me. They wanted me to move fast, and if
anything can stir a guy up it's getting shot at. If I had anything to hide or to work at, it would come out in a hurry."

"But you didn't bring anything out?"

I grinned at him and I could see my reflection in the
glass facing of the autographed pictures behind his head.
It wasn't a pretty face at all, teeth and hate and some
wildness hard to describe. "No, I didn't. So now I'm a
real target because I know too much. They know I *don't*
have Velda's location and from now on I can only be
trouble to them. I'll bet you that right now a hunt is on
for me."

"Mike—if you called Pat—"

"Come off it. He's no friend anymore. He'll do anything
to nail my ass down and don't you forget it."

"Does he know the facts?"

"No. The hell with him."

Hy pushed his glasses up on his head, frowning. "Well,
what are you going to do?"

"Do, old buddy? I'll tell you what I'm going to do. I'm

going after the missing piece. If I weren't so damn slow after all those years I would have caught it before. I'm going after the facts that can wrap up the ball game and you're going with me."

"But you said—"

"Uh-uh. I didn't say anything. I *don't* know where she is, but I do know a few other things. Richie Cole came blasting back into this country when he shouldn't have and ducked out to look for me. That had a big fat meaning and I muffed it. Damn it, I muffed it!"

"But how?"

"Come on, Hy—Richie was a sailor—he smuggled her on the ship he came in on. *He never left her in Europe! He got her back in this country!*"

He put the cigar down slowly, getting the implication.

I said, "He had to smuggle her out, otherwise they would have killed her. If they took a plane they would have blown it over the ocean, or if she sailed under an assumed name and cover identity they would have had enough time to locate her and a passenger would simply fall overboard. No, he smuggled her out. He got her on that ship and got her into this country."

"You make it sound easy."

"Sure it's easy! You think there wasn't some cooperation with others in the crew! Those boys love to outfox the captain and the customs. What would they care as long as it was on Cole's head? He was on a tramp steamer and they can do practically anything on those babies if they know how and want to. Look, you want me to cite you examples?"

"I know it could be done."

"All right, then here's the catch. Richie realized how close The Dragon was to Velda when they left. He had no time. He had to act on his own. This was a project bigger than any going in the world at the time, big enough to break regulations for. He got her out—but he didn't underestimate the enemy either. He knew they'd figure it and be waiting.

"They were, too," I continued. "The Dragon was there

all right, and he followed Cole thinking he was going to an appointed place where he had already hidden Velda, but when he realized that Cole wasn't doing anything of the kind he figured the angles quickly. He shot Cole, had to leave because of the crowd that collected and didn't have a chance until later to reach Old Dewey, then found out about me. Don't ask me the details about *how* they can do it—they have resources at their fingertips everywhere. Later he went back, killed Dewey, didn't find the note Cole left and had to stick with me to see where I led him."

Hy was frowning again.

I said, "I couldn't lead him to Velda. I didn't know. But before long he'll figure out the same thing I did. Somebody else helped Cole get her off that boat and knows where she is!"

"What are you going to do?" His voice was quietly calm next to mine.

"Get on that ship and see who else was in on the deal."

"How?"

"Be my guest and I'll show you the seamier side of life."

"You know me," Hy said, standing up.

I paid the cabbie outside Benny Joe Grissi's bar and when Hy saw where we were he let out a low whistle and said he hoped I knew what I was doing. We went inside and Sugar Boy and his smaller friend were still at their accustomed places and when Sugar Boy saw me he got a little pasty around the mouth and looked toward the bar with a quick motion of his head.

Benny Joe gave the nod and we walked past without saying a word, and when I got to the bar I held out the card Art Rickerby had given me and let Benny Joe take a long look at it. "In case you get ideas like before, mister. I'll shoot this place apart and you with it."

"Say, Mike, I never—"

"Tone it down," I said. "Bayliss Henry here?"

"Pepper? Yeah. He went in the can."

"Wait here, Hy."

I went down the end to the door stenciled MEN and

pushed on in. Old Bayliss was at the washstand drying his hands and saw me in the mirror, his eyes suddenly wary at the recognition. He turned around and put his hands on my chest. "Mike, my boy, no more. Whatever it is, I want none of it. The last time out taught me a lesson I won't forget. I'm old, I scare easy, and what life is left to me I want to enjoy. Okay?"

"Sure."

"Then forget whatever you came in here to ask me. Don't let me talk over my head about the old days or try and make like a reporter again."

"You won't get shot at."

Bayliss nodded and shrugged. "How can I argue with you? What do you want to know?"

"What ship was Richie Cole on?"

"The *Vanessa*."

"What pier?"

"She was at number twelve, but that won't do you any good now."

"Why not?"

"Hell, she sailed the day before yesterday."

What I had to say I did under my breath. Everything was right out the window because I thought too slow and a couple of days had made all the difference.

"What was on it, Mike?"

"I wanted to see a guy."

"Oh? I thought it was the ship. Well maybe you can still see some of the guys. You know the *Vanessa* was the ship they had the union trouble with. Everybody complained about the chow and half the guys wouldn't sign back on. The union really laid into 'em."

Then suddenly there was a chance again and I had to grab at it. "Listen, Bayliss—who did Cole hang around with on the ship?"

"Jeepers, Mike, out at sea—"

"Did he have any friends on board?"

"Well, no, I'd say."

"Come on, damn it, a guy doesn't sail for months and not make some kind of an acquaintance!"

"Yeah, I know—well, Cole was a chess player and there was this one guy—let's see, Red Markham—yeah, that's it, Red Markham. They'd have drinks together and play chess together because Red sure could play chess. One time—"

"Where can I find this guy?"

"You know where Annie Stein's pad is?"

"The flophouse?"

"Yeah. Well, you look for him there. He gets drunk day-times and flops early."

"Suppose you go along."

"Mike, I told you—"

"Hy Gardner's outside."

Bayliss looked up and grinned. "Well, shoot. If he's along I'll damn well go. He was still running copy when I did the police beat."

Annie Stein's place was known as the Harbor Hotel. It was a dollar a night flop, pretty expensive as flops go, so the trade was limited to occasional workers and itinerant seamen. It was old and dirty and smelled of disinfectant and urine partially smothered by an old-man odor of defeat and decay.

The desk clerk froze when we walked in, spun the book around without asking, not wanting any trouble at all. Red Markham was in the third room on the second floor, his door half open, the sound and smell of him oozing into the corridor.

I pushed the door open and flipped on the light. Overhead a sixty-watt bulb turned everything yellow. He was curled on the cot, an empty pint bottle beside him, breathing heavily through his mouth. On the chair with his jacket and hat was a pocket-sized chessboard with pegged chessmen arranged in some intricate move.

It took ten minutes of cold wet towels and a lot of shaking to wake him up. His eyes still had a whiskey glassiness and he didn't know what we wanted at all. He was unintelligible for another thirty minutes, then little by little he began to come around, his face going through a succession of emotions. Until he saw Bayliss he seemed scared, but one look at the old man and he tried on a drunken grin, gagged and went into a spasm of dry heaves. Luckily, there was nothing in his stomach, so we didn't have to go through that kind of mess.

Hy brought in a glass of water and I made him sip at it. I said, "What's your name, feller?"

He hiccoughed. "You—cops?"

"No, a friend."

"Oh." His head wobbled, then he looked back to me again. "You play chess?"

"Sorry, Red, but I had a friend who could. Richie Cole."

Markham squinted and nodded solemnly, remembering. "He—pretty damn good. Yessir. Good guy."

I asked him, "Did you know about the girl on the ship?"

Very slowly, he scowled, his lips pursing out, then a bit of clarity returned to him and he leered with a drunken grimace. "Sure. Hell of—joke." He hiccoughed and grinned again. "Joke. Hid—her in—down in—hold."

We were getting close now. His eyes drooped sleepily and I wanted him to hang on. I said, "Where is she now, Red?"

He just looked at me foggily.

"Damn it, think about it!"

For a second he didn't like the way I yelled or my hand on his arm and he was about to balk, then Bayliss said, "Come on, Red, if you know where she is, tell us."

You'd think he was seeing Bayliss for the first time. "Pepper," he said happily, his eyes coming open.

"Come on, Red. The girl on the *Vanessa*. Richie's girl."

"Sure. Big—joke. You know?"

"We know, but tell us where she is."

His shrug was the elaborate gesture of the sodden drunk. "Dunno. I—got her—on deck."

Bayliss looked at me, not knowing where to go. It was all over his head and he was taking the lead from me. Then he got the pitch and shook Red's shoulder. "Is she on shore?"

Red chuckled and his head weaved. "On—shore. Sure—

on shore." He laughed again, the picture coming back to his mind. "Dennis—Wallace packed her—in crate. Very funny."

I pushed Bayliss away and sat on the edge of the cot. "It sure was a good joke all right. Now where did the crate go?"

"Crate?"

"She was packed in the crate. This Dennis Wallace packed her in the crate, right?"

"Right!" he said assuredly, slobbering on himself.

"Then who got the crate?"

"Big joke."

"I know, now let us in on it. Who got the crate?"

He made another one of those shrugs. "I—dunno."

"Somebody picked it up," I reminded him.

Red's smile was real foolish, that of the drunk trying to be secretive. "Richie's—joke. He called—a friend. Dennis gave him—the crate." He laughed again. "Very funny."

Hy said, "Cute."

I nodded. "Yeah. Now we have to find this Dennis guy."

"He's got a place not far from here," Bayliss said.

"You know everybody?"

"I've been around a long time, Mike."

We went to leave Red Markham sitting there, but before we could reach the door he called out, "Hey, you."

Bayliss said, "What, Red?"

"How come—everybody wants—old Dennis?"

"I don't—"

My hand stopped the old guy and I walked back to the cot. "Who else wanted Dennis, Red?"

"Guy—gimme this pint." He reached for the bottle, but was unable to make immediate contact. When he did he sucked at the mouth of it, swallowed as though it was filled and put the bottle down.

"What did he look like, Red?"

"Oh—" he lolled back against the wall. "Big guy. Like you."

"Go on."

"Mean. Son of a—he was mean. You ever see—mean

ones? Like a damn Indian. Something like Injun Pete on the *Darby Standard*—he—"

I didn't bother to hear him finish. I looked straight at Hy and felt cold all over. "The Dragon," I said. "He's one step up."

Hy had a quiet look on his face. "That's what I almost forgot to tell you about, Mike."

"What?"

"The Dragon. I got inside the code name from our people overseas. There may be two guys because The Dragon code breaks down to *tooth* and *nail*. When they operate as a team they're simply referred to as The Dragon."

"Great," I said. "Swell. That's all we need for odds." My mouth had a bad taste in it. "Show us Dennis's place, Bayliss. We can't stay here any longer."

"Not me," he said. "You guys go it alone. Whatever it is that's going on, I don't like it. I'll tell you where, but I'm not going in any more dark places with you. Right now I'm going back to Benny Joe Grissi's bar and get stinking drunk where you can't get at me and if anything happens I'll read about it in the papers tomorrow."

"Good enough, old-timer. Now where does Dennis live?"

The rooming house was a brownstone off Ninth Avenue, a firetrap like all the others on the block, a crummy joint filled with cubicles referred to as furnished rooms. The landlady came out of the front floor flat, looked at me and said, "I don't want no cops around here," and when Hy handed her the ten-spot her fat face made a brief smile and she added, "So I made a mistake. Cops don't give away the green. What're you after?"

"Dennis Wallace. He's a seaman and—"

"Top floor front. Go on up. He's got company."

I flashed Hy a nod, took the stairs with him behind me while I yanked the .45 out and reached the top floor in seconds. The old carpet under our feet puffed dust with every step but muffled them effectively and when I reached the door there was no sound from within and a pencil-thin line of light seeped out at the sill. I tried the knob, pushed the door open and was ready to cut loose at anything that moved wrong.

But there was no need for any shooting, if the little guy on the floor with his hands tied behind him and his throat slit wide open was Dennis Wallace, for his killer was long gone.

The fat landlady screeched when she saw the body and told us it was Dennis all right. She waddled downstairs again and pointed to the wall phone and after trying four different numbers I got Pat and told him I was with another dead man. It wasn't anything startling, he was very proper about getting down the details and told me to stay right there. His voice had a fine tone of satisfaction to it that said he had me where he could make me sweat and maybe even break me like he had promised.

Hy came down as I hung up and tapped my shoulder. "You didn't notice something on the guy up there."

"What's that?"

"All that blood didn't come from his throat. His gut is all carved up and his mouth is taped shut. The blood obscures the tape."

"Tortured?"

"It sure looks that way."

The landlady was in her room taking a quick shot for her nerves and seemed to hate us for causing all the trouble. I asked her when Dennis' guest had arrived and she said a couple of hours ago. She hadn't heard him leave so she assumed he was still there. Her description was brief, but enough. He was a big mean-looking guy who reminded her of an Indian.

There was maybe another minute before a squad car would come along and I didn't want to be here when that happened. I pulled Hy out on the stoop and said, "I'm going to take off."

"Pat won't like it."

"There isn't time to talk about it. You can give him the poop."

"All of it?"

"Every bit. Lay it out for him."

"What about you?"

"Look, you saw what happened. The Dragon put it together the same way I did. He was here when the boat docked and Richie Cole knew it. So Richie called for a friend who knew the ropes, told him to pick up the crate with Velda in it and where to bring it. He left and figured right when he guessed anybody waiting would follow him. He pulled them away from the boat and tried to make contact with Old Dewey at the newstand and what he had for Dewey was the location of where that friend was to bring the crate."

"Then there's one more step."

"That's right. The friend."

"You can't trace that call after all this time."

"I don't think I have to."

Hy shook his head. "If Cole was a top agent then he didn't have any friends."

"He had one," I said.

"Who?"

"Velda."

"But—"

"So he could just as well have another. Someone who was in the same game with him during the war, someone he knew would realize the gravity of the situation and act immediately and someone he knew would be capable of fulfilling the mission."

"Who, Mike?"

I didn't tell him. "I'll call you when it's over. You tell Pat."

Down the street a squad car turned the corner. I went down the steps and went in the other direction, walking casually, then when I reached Ninth, I flagged a cab and gave him the parking lot where I had left Laura's car.

CHAPTER 12

If I was wrong, the girl hunters would have Velda. She'd be dead. They wanted nothing of her except that she be dead. Damn their stinking hides anyway. Damn them and their philosophies! Death and destruction were the only things the Kremlin crowd was capable of. They knew the value of violence and death and used it over and over in a wild scheme to smash everything flat but their own kind.

But there was one thing they didn't know. They didn't know how to handle it when it came back to them and exploded in their own faces. Let her be dead, *I thought,* and I'll start a hunt of my own. They think *they* can hunt? Shit. They didn't know how to be *really* violent. Death? I'd get them, every one, no matter how big or little, or wherever they were. I'd cut them down like so many grapes in ways that would scare the living crap out of them and those next in line for my kill would never know a second's peace until their heads went flying every which way.

So I'd better not be wrong.

Dennis Wallace had known who was to pick up the crate. There wouldn't have been time for elaborate exchanges of coded recognition signals and if Dennis had known it was more than just a joke he might conceivably have backed out. No, it had to be quick and simple and not at all frightening. He had turned the crate over to a guy whose name had been given him and since it was big enough a truck would have been used in the delivery. He would have seen lettering on the truck, he would have been able to identify both it and the driver, and with some judicious knife work on his belly he would have had his memory jarred into remembering every single detail of the transaction.

I had to be right.

Art Rickerby had offered the clue.

The guy's name had to be Alex Bird, Richie's old war buddy in the O.S.S. who had a chicken farm up in Marlboro, New York, and who most likely had a pickup truck that could transport a crate. He would do the favor, keep his mouth shut and forget it the way he had been trained to, and it was just as likely he missed any newspaper squibs about Richie's death and so didn't show up to talk to the police when Richie was killed.

By the time I reached the George Washington Bridge the stars were wiped out of the night sky and you could smell the rain again. I took the Palisades Drive and where I turned off to pick up the Thruway the rain came down in fine slanting lines that laid a slick on the road and whipped in the window.

I liked a night like this. It could put a quiet on everything. Your feet walked softer and dogs never barked in the rain. It obscured visibility and overrode sounds that could give you away otherwise and sometimes was so soothing that you could be lulled into a death sleep. Yeah, I remembered other nights like this too. Death nights.

At Newburgh I turned off the Thruway, drove down 17K into town and turned north on 9W. I stopped at a gas station when I reached Marlboro and asked the attendant if he knew where Alex Bird lived.

Yes, he knew. He pointed the way out and just to be sure I sketched out the route then picked up the blacktop road that led back into the country.

I passed by it the first time, turned around at the cross-road cursing to myself, then eased back up the road look-

ing for the mailbox. There was no name on it, just a big
wooden cutout of a bird. It was in the shadow of a tree
before, but now my lights picked it out and when they
did I spotted the drive, turned in, angled off into a cut in
the bushes and killed the engine.

The farmhouse stood an eighth of a mile back off the
road, an old building restored to more modern taste. In
back of it, dimly lit by the soft glow of night lights, were
two long chicken houses, the manure odor of them hanging in the wet air. On the right, a hundred feet away, a
two-story boxlike barn stood in deep shadow, totally dark.

Only one light was on in the house when I reached it,
downstairs on the chimney side and obviously in a living
room. I held there a minute, letting my eyes get adjusted to
the place. There were no cars around, but that didn't count
since there were too many places to hide one. I took out the
.45, jacked a shell in the chamber and thumbed the hammer back.

But before I could move another light went on in the
opposite downstairs room. Behind the curtains a shadow
moved slowly, purposefully, passed the window several
times then disappeared altogether. I waited, but the light
didn't go out. Instead, one top-floor light came on, but too
dimly to do more than vaguely outline the form of a person
on the curtains.

Then it suddenly made sense to me and I ran across the
distance to the door. Somebody was searching the house.

The door was locked and too heavy to kick in. I hoped
the rain covered the racket I made, then laid my trench
coat against the window and pushed. The glass shattered
inward to the carpeted floor without much noise, I undid
the catch, lifted the window and climbed over the sill.

Alex Bird would be the thin, balding guy tied to the
straightback chair. His head slumped forward, his chin on
his chest and when I tilted his head back his eyes stared
at me lifelessly. There was a small lumpy bruise on the
side of his head where he had been hit, but outside of a
chafing of his wrists and ankles, there were no other marks
on him. His body had the warmth of death only a few

minutes old and I had seen too many heart-attack cases not to be able to diagnose this one.

The Dragon had reached Alex Bird, all right. He had him right where he could make him talk and the little guy's heart exploded on him. That meant just one thing. He hadn't talked. The Dragon was still searching. *He didn't know where she was yet!*

And right then, right that very second he was upstairs tearing the house apart!

The stairs were at a shallow angle reaching to the upper landing and I hugged the wall in the shadows until I could definitely place him from the sounds. I tried to keep from laughing out loud because I felt so good, and although I could hold back the laugh I couldn't suppress the grin. I could feel it stretch my face and felt the pull across my shoulders and back, then I got ready to go.

I knew when he felt it. When death is your business you have a feeling for it; an animal instinct can tell when it's close even when you can't see it or hear it. You just know it's there. And like he knew suddenly that I was there, I realized he knew it too.

Upstairs the sounds stopped abruptly. There was the smallest of metallic *clicks* that could have been made by a gun, but that was all. Both of us were waiting. Both of us knew we wouldn't wait long.

You can't play games when time is so important. You take a chance on being hit and maybe living through it just so you get one clean shot in where it counts. You have to end the play knowing one must die and sometimes two and there's no other way. For the first time you both know it's pro against pro, two cold, calm killers facing each other down and there's no such thing as sportsmanship and if an advantage is offered it will be taken and whoever offered it will be dead.

We came around the corners simultaneously with the rolling thunder of the .45 blanking out the rod in his hand and I felt a sudden torch along my side and another on my arm. It was immediate and unaimed diversionary fire until you could get the target lined up and in the space of four rapid-fire shots I saw him, huge at the top of the stairs, his high-cheek-boned face truly Indianlike, the black hair low on his forehead and his mouth twisted open in the sheer enjoyment of what he was doing.

Then my shot slammed the gun out of his hand and the advantage was his because he was up there, a crazy killer with a scream on his lips and like the animal he was he reacted instantly and dove headlong at me through the acrid fumes of the gunsmoke.

The impact knocked me flat on my back, smashing into a corner table so that the lamp shattered into a million pieces beside my head. I had my hands on him, his coat tore, a long tattered slice of it in my fingers, then he kicked free with a snarl and a guttural curse, rolling to his feet like an acrobat. The .45 had skittered out of my hand and lay up against the step. All it needed was a quick movement and it was mine. He saw the action, figured the odds and knew he couldn't reach me before I had the gun, and while I grabbed it up he was into the living room and out the front door. The slide was forward and the hammer back so there was still one shot left at least and he couldn't afford the chance of losing. I saw his blurred shadow racing toward the drive and when my shadow broke the shaft of light coming from the door he swerved into the darkness of the barn and I let a shot go at him and heard it smash into the woodwork.

It was my last. This time the slide stayed back. I dropped the gun in the grass, ran to the barn before he could pull the door closed and dived into the darkness.

He was on me like a cat, but he made a mistake in reaching for my right hand thinking I had the gun there. I got the other hand in his face and damn near tore it off. He didn't yell. He made a sound deep in his throat and went for my neck. He was big and strong and wild mean, but it was my kind of game too. I heaved up and threw him off, got to my feet and kicked out to where he was. I missed my aim, but my toe took him in the side and he grunted and came back with a vicious swipe of his hand I could only partially block. I felt his next move coming and let an old-time reflex take over. The judo bit is great if everything is going for you, but a terrible right cross to the face can destroy judo or karate or anything else if it gets there first.

My hand smashed into bone and flesh and with the meaty impact I could smell the blood and hear the gagging intake of his breath. He grabbed, his arms like great claws. He just held on and I knew if I couldn't break him loose he could kill me. He figured I'd start the knee coming up and turned to block it with a half-turn. But I did something worse, I grabbed him with my hands, squeezed and twisted and his scream was like a woman's, so high-pitched as almost to be noiseless, and in his frenzy of pain he shoved me so violently I lost that fanatical hold of what manhood I had left him, and with some blind hate driving him he came at me as I stumbled over something and fell on me like a wild beast, his teeth tearing at me, his hands searching and ripping and I felt the shock of incredible pain and ribs break under his pounding and I couldn't get him off no matter what I did, and he was holding me down and butting me with his head while he kept up that whistle-like screaming and in another minute it would be me dead and him alive, then Velda dead.

And when I thought of her name something happened, that little thing you have left over was there and I got my elbow up, smashed his head back unexpectedly, got a short one to his jaw again, then another, and another, and another, then I was on top of him and hitting, hitting, smashing—and he wasn't moving at all under me. He was breathing, but not moving.

I got up and found the doorway somehow, standing there to suck in great breaths of air. I could feel the blood running from my mouth and nose, wetting my shirt, and with each breath my side would wrench and tear. The two bullet burns were nothing compared to the rest. I had been squeezed dry, pulled apart, almost destroyed, but I had won. Now the son of a bitch would die.

Inside the door I found a light switch. It only threw on a small bulb overhead, but it was enough. I walked back to where he lay face up and then spat down on The Dragon. Mechanically, I searched his pockets, found nothing except money until I saw that one of my fists had torn his hair loose at the side and when I ripped the wig off there were several small strips of microfilm hidden there.

Hell, I didn't know what they were. I didn't care. I even grinned at the slob because he sure did look like an Indian now, only one that had been half scalped by an amateur. He was big, big. Cheekbones high, a Slavic cast to his eyes, his mouth a cruel slash, his eyebrows thick and black. Half bald, though, he wouldn't have looked too much like an Indian. Not our kind, anyway.

There was an ax on the wall, a long-handled, double-bitted ax with a finely honed edge and I picked it from the pegs and went back to The Dragon.

Just how *did* you kill a dragon? I could bury the ax in his belly. That would be fun, all right. Stick it right in the middle of his skull and it would look at lot better. They wouldn't come fooling around after seeing pictures of that. How about the neck? One whack and his head would roll like the Japs used to do. But nuts, why be that kind?

This guy was *really* going to die.

I looked at the big pig, put the ax down and nudged him with my toe. What was it Art had said? Like about suffering? I thought he was nuts, but he could be right. Yeah, he sure could be right. Still, there had to be some indication that people were left who treat those Commie slobs like they liked to treat people.

Some indication.

He was Gorlin now, Comrade Gorlin. Dragons just aren't dragons anymore when they're bubbling blood over their chins.

I walked around the building looking for an *indication*. I found it on a workbench in the back.

A twenty-penny nail and a ball peen hammer. The nail seemed about four inches long and the head big as a dime.

I went back and turned Comrade Gorlin over on his face.

I stretched his arm out palm down on the floor.

I tapped the planks until I found a floor beam and put his hand on it.

It was too bad he wasn't conscious.

Then I held the nail in the middle of the back of his hand and slammed it in with the hammer and slammed and slammed and slammed until the head of that nail dimpled his skin and he was so tightly pinned to the floor like a piece of equipment he'd never get loose until he was pried out and he wasn't going to do it with a ball peen. I threw the hammer down beside him and said, "Better'n handcuffs, buddy," but he didn't get the joke. He was still out.

Outside, the rain came down harder. It always does after a thing like that, trying to flush away the memory of it. I picked up my gun, took it in the house and dismantled it, wiped it dry and reassembled the piece.

Only then did I walk to the telephone and ask the operator to get me New York and the number I gave her was that of the Peerage Brokers.

Art Rickerby answered the phone himself. He said, "Mike?"

"Yes."

For several seconds there was silence. "Mike—"

"I have him for you. He's still alive."

It was as though I had merely told him the time. "Thank you," he said.

"You'll cover for me on this."

"It will be taken care of. Where is he?"

I told him. I gave him the story then too. I told him to call Pat and Hy and let it all loose at once. Everything tied in. It was almost all wrapped up.

Art said, "One thing, Mike."

"What?"

"*Your* problem."

"No trouble. It's over. I was standing here cleaning my gun and it all was like snapping my fingers. It was simple. If I had thought of it right away Dewey and Dennis Wallace and Alex Bird would still be alive. It was tragically simple. I could have found out where Velda was days ago."

"Mike—"

"I'll see you, Art. The rest of The Dragon has yet to fall."

"What?" He didn't understand me.

"*Tooth and Nail.* I just got Tooth— Nail is more subtle."

"We're going to need a statement."

"You'll get it."

"How will—"

I interrupted him with, "I'll call you."

CHAPTER 13

At daylight the rain stopped and the music of sunlight played off the trees and grass at dawn. The mountains glittered and shone and steamed a little, and as the sun rose the sheen stopped and the colors came through. I ate at an all-night drive-in, parking between the semis out front. I sat through half a dozen cups of coffee before paying the bill and going out to the day, ignoring the funny looks of the carhop.

I stopped again awhile by the Ashokan Reservoir and did nothing but look at the water and try to bring seven years into focus. It was a long time, that. You change in seven years.

You change in seven days too, I thought.

I was a bum Pat had dragged into a hospital to look at a dying man. Pat didn't know it, but I was almost as dead as the one on the bed. It depends on where you die. My dying had been almost done. The drying up, the withering, had taken place. Everything was gone except hopelessness and that is the almost death of living.

Remember, Velda, when we were big together? You must have remembered or you would never have asked for me. And all these years I had spent trying to forget you while you were trying to remember me.

I got up slowly and brushed off my pants, then walked back across the field to the car. During the night I had gotten it all muddy driving aimlessly on the back roads, but I didn't think Laura would mind.

The sun had climbed high until it was almost directly overhead. When you sit and think time can go by awfully fast. I turned the key, pulled out on the road and headed toward the mountains.

When I drove up, Laura heard me coming and ran out to meet me. She came into my arms with a rush of pure delight and did nothing for a few seconds except hold her arms around me, then she looked again, stepped back and said, "Mike—your face!"

"Trouble, baby. I told you I was trouble."

For the first time I noticed my clothes. My coat swung open and there was blood down my jacket and shirt and a jagged tear that was clotted with more blood at my side.

Her eyes went wide, not believing what she saw. "Mike! You're—you're all—"

"Shot down, kid. Rough night."

She shook her head. "It's not funny. I'm going to call a doctor!"

I took her hand. "No, you're not. It isn't that bad."

"Mike—"

"Favor, kitten. Let me lie in the sun like an old dog, okay? I don't want a damn medic. I'll heal. It's happened before. I just want to be left alone in the sun."

"Oh, Mike, you stubborn fool."

"Anybody home?" I asked her.

"No, you always pick an off day for the servants." She smiled again now. "You're clever and I'm glad."

I nodded. For some reason my side had started to ache and it was getting hard to breathe. There were other places that had pain areas all their own and they weren't going to get better. It had only just started. I said, "I'm tired."

So we went out back to the pool. She helped me off with my clothes and once more I put the trunks on, then eased down into a plastic contour chair and let the sun warm me.

There were blue marks from my shoulders down and where the rib was broken a welt had raised, an angry red that arched from front to back. Laura found antiseptic and cleaned out the furrow where the two shots had grazed me and I thought back to the moment of getting them, realizing how lucky I was because the big jerk was too impatient, just like I had been, taking too much pleasure out of something that should have been strictly business.

I slept for a while. I felt the sun travel across my body from one side to the other, then I awoke abruptly because events had compacted themselves into my thoughts and I knew that there was still that one thing more to do.

Laura said, "You were talking in your sleep, Mike."

She had changed back into that black bikini and it was wet like her skin so she must have just come from the water. The tight band of black at her loins had rolled down some from the swim and fitted tightly into the crevasses of her body. The top half was like an artist's brush stroke, a quick motion of impatience at a critical sex-conscious world that concealed by reason of design only. She was more nearly naked dressed than nude.

How lovely.

Large, flowing thighs. Full, round calves. They blended into a softly concave stomach and emerged, higher, into proud, outthrust breasts. Her face and hair were a composite halo reaching for the perfection of beauty and she was smiling.

Lovely.

"What did I say, Laura?"

She stopped smiling then. "You were talking about dragons."

I nodded. "Today, I'm St. George."

"Mike—"

"Sit down, baby."

"Can we talk again?"

"Yes, we'll talk."

"Would you mind if I got dressed first? It's getting chilly out here now. You ought to get dressed yourself."

She was right. The sun was a thick red now, hanging

just over the crest of a mountain. While one side was a blaze of green, the other was in the deep purple of the shadow.

I held out my hand and she helped me up, and together we walked around the pool to the bathhouse, touching each other, feeling the warmth of skin against skin, the motion of muscle against muscle. At the door she turned and I took her in my arms. "Back to back?" she said.

"Like prudes," I told her.

Her eyes grew soft and her lips wet her tongue. Slowly, with an insistent hunger, her mouth turned up to mine and I took it, tasting her again, knowing her, feeling the surge of desire go through me and through her too.

I let her go reluctantly and she went inside with me behind her. The setting sun threw long orange rays through the window, so there was no need of the overhead light. She went into the shower and turned on a soft drizzle while I got dressed slowly, aching and hurting as I pulled on my clothes.

She called out, "When will it all be over, Mike?"

"Today," I said quietly.

"Today?"

I heard her stop soaping herself in the shower. "Are you sure?"

"Yes."

"You were dreaming about dragons," she called out.

"About how they die, honey. They die hard. This one will die especially hard. You know, you wouldn't believe how things come about. Things that were planted long ago suddenly bear fruit now. Like what I told you. Remember all I told you about Velda?"

"Yes, Mike, I do."

"I had to revise and add to the story, Laura."

"Really?" She turned the shower off and stood there behind me soaping herself down, the sound of it so nice and natural I wanted to turn around and watch. I knew what she'd look like: darkly beautiful, blondely beautiful, the sun having turned all of her hair white.

I said, "Pat was right and I was right. Your jewels did

come into it. They were like Mrs. Civac's jewels and the fact that Richie Cole was a jewel smuggler."

"Oh?" That was all she said.

"They were all devices. Decoys. Red herrings. How would you like to hear the rest of what I think?"

"All right, Mike."

She didn't see me, but I nodded. "In the government are certain key men. Their importance is apparent to critical eyes long before it is to the public. Your husband was like that. It was evident that he was going to be a top dog one day and the kind of top dog our Red enemy could hardly afford to have up there.

"That was Leo Knapp, your husband. Mr. Missile Man. Mr. America. He sure was a big one. But our wary enemy knew his stuff. Kill him off and you had a public martyr or a great investigation that might lead to even greater international stuff and those Reds just aren't the kind who can stand the big push. Like it or not, they're still a lousy bunch of peasants who killed to control but who can be knocked into line by the likes of us. They're shouting slobs who'll run like hell when class shows and they know this inside their feeble little heads. So they didn't want Leo Knapp put on a pedestal.

"Control comes other ways, however. For instance, he could marry a woman who would listen to him as a sounding board and relay his thoughts and secrets to the right persons so that whatever he did could be quickly annulled by some other action. He could marry a woman who, as his official Washington hostess, had the ear of respected persons and could pick up things here and there that were as important to enemy ears as any sealed documents. He could find his work being stymied at every turn.

"Then one day he figured it all out. He pinpointed the enemy and found it within his own house. He baited a trap by planting supposedly important papers in his safe and one night while the enemy, his wife, was rifling his safe with her compatriot who was to photograph the papers and transport the photos to higher headquarters, he came downstairs. He saw her, accused her, but blundered into a game bigger than he was.

"Let's say she shot him. It doesn't really matter. She was just as guilty even if it was the other one. At least the other one carried the gun off—a pickup rod traceable to no one if it was thrown away printless. His wife delayed long enough so she and her compatriot could fake a robbery, let the guy get away, then call in the cops.

"Nor does it end there. The same wife still acts as the big Washington hostess with her same ear to the same ground and is an important and inexhaustible supply of information to the enemy. Let's say that she is so big as to even be part of The Dragon team. He was Tooth, she was Nail, both spies, both assassins, both deadly enemies of this country."

Behind me the water went on again, a downpour that would rinse the bubbles of soap from her body.

"All went well until Richie Cole was killed. Tooth went and used the same gun again. It tied things in. Like I told you when I let you be *my* sounding board—coincidence is a strange thing. I like the word 'fate' even better. Or is 'consequence' an even better one? Richie and Leo and Velda were all tied into the same big situation and for a long time I was too damn dumb to realize it.

"A guy like me doesn't stay dumb forever, though. Things change. You either die or smarten up. I had The Dragon on my back and when I think about it all the little things make sense too. At least I think so. Remember how when Gorlin shot the radio you shook with what I thought was fear? Hell, baby, that was rage. You were pissed off that he could pull such a stupid stunt and maybe put your hide in danger. Later you gave him hell on the phone, didn't you? That house is like an echo chamber, baby. Talk downstairs and you hear the tones all over. You were mad. I was too interested in going through your husband's effects to pay any attention, that was all.

"Now it's over. Tooth is nailed, but that's a joke you don't understand yet, baby. Let's just say that The Dragon is tethered. He'll sit in the chair and all the world will know why and nations will backtrack and lie and propaganda will tear up the knotheads in the Kremlin and maybe their satellite countries will wise up and blast loose and maybe we'll wise up and blast them, but however it goes, The Dragon is dead. It didn't find Velda. She'll talk, she'll open up the secrets of the greatest espionage organization the world has ever known and Communist philosophy will get the hell knocked out of it.

"You see, baby, I know where Velda is."

The shower stopped running and I could hear her hum as though she couldn't even hear me.

"The catch was this. Richie Cole did make his contact. He gave Old Dewey, the newsstand operator, a letter he had that told where Alex Bird would take Velda. It was a prepared place and she had orders to stay there until either he came for her or I came for her. He'll never come for her.

"Only me," I said. "Dewey put the letter in a magazine. Every month he holds certain magazines aside for me and to make sure I got it he put it inside my copy of *Cavalier*. It will be there when I go back to the city. I'll pick it up and it will tell me where Velda is."

I finished dressing, put on the empty gun and slid painfully into the jacket. The blood was crusty on my clothes, but it really didn't matter anymore.

I said, "It's all speculation. I might be wrong. I just can't take any chances. I've loved other women. I loved Velda. I've loved you and like you said, it's either you or her. I have to go for her, you know that. If she's alive I have to find her. The key is right there inside my copy of that magazine. It will have my name on it and Duck-Duck will hand it over and I'll know where she is."

She stopped humming and I knew she was listening. I heard her make a curious woman-sound like a sob.

"I may be wrong, Laura. I may see her and not want her. I may be wrong about you, and if I am I'll be back, but I have to find out." The slanting beam of the sun struck the other side of the bathhouse leaving me in the shadow then. I knew what I had to do. It had to be a test.

They either passed it or failed it. No in-betweens. I didn't want it on my head again.

I reached for the shotgun in the corner, turned it upside down and shoved the barrels deep into the blue clay and twisted them until I was sure both barrels were plugged just like a cookie cutter and I left it lying there and opened the door.

The mountains were in deep shadow, the sun out of sight and only its light flickering off the trees. It was a hundred miles into the city, but I'd take the car again and it wouldn't really be very long at all. I'd see Pat and we'd be friends again and Hy would get his story and Velda— Velda? What would it be like now?

I started up the still wet concrete walk away from the bathhouse and she called out, "Mike—*Mike!*"

I turned at the sound of her voice and there she stood in the naked, glossy, shimmering beauty of womanhood, the lovely tan of her skin blossoming and swelling in all the vast hillocks and curves that make a woman, the glinting blond hair throwing tiny lights back into the sunset and over it all those incredible gray eyes.

Incredible.

They watched me over the elongated barrels of the shotgun and seemed to twinkle and swirl in the fanatical delight of murder they come up with at the moment of the kill, the moment of truth.

But for whom? Truth will out, but for whom?

The muzzle of the gun was a pair of yawning chasms but there was no depth to their mouths. Down the length of the blued steel the blood crimson of her nails made a startling and symbolic contrast.

Death red, I thought. The fingers behind them should have been tan but weren't. They were a tense, drawing white and with another fraction of an inch the machinery of the gun would go into motion.

She said, "Mike—" and in that one word there was hate and desire, revenge and regret, but above all the timbre of duty long ago instilled into a truly mechanical mind.

I said, "So long, baby."

Then I turned and walked toward the outside and Velda and behind me I heard the unearthly roar as she pulled both triggers at once.

Other SIGNET Fiction You'll Enjoy

One Flew Over the Cuckoo's Nest *by Ken Kesey.* A powerful novel about a boisterous rebel who swaggers into the ward of a mental hospital and takes over. (#T2240—75¢)

Twilight of Honor *by Al Dewlen.* A high-tension drama about a vicious murder and a sensational courtroom trial. This bestseller was a Book-of-the-Month Club selection in its hardbound edition. (#T2257—75¢)

Uptown Downtown *by Dennis Lynds.* A conservative by day . . . a beatnik by night . . . Dave Garber makes the best of both worlds, until forced to choose between them. (#D2267—50¢)

Portrait of a Young Man Drowning *by Charles Perry.* The harrowing story of how a decent young man turns into a vicious psychopath. (#T2248—75¢)

The Agony and the Ecstasy *by Irving Stone.* The big bestseller based on the life of Michaelangelo, the brilliant and lusty Renaissance sculptor and painter. (#Q2246—95¢)

Wilderness *by Robert Penn Warren.* A stirring Civil War story about a man who leaves a Bavarian ghetto to join the Union Army. (#P2231—60¢)

Climate of Violence *by Russell O'Neil.* A frank, disturbing novel about what happens to an ordinary family when three young boys commit a senselessly brutal crime. (#T2188—75¢)

Lan-Lan *by Harry Roskolenko.* Set in exotic Cambodia, the story of an ambitious French doctor and the beautiful concubine he loves but will not marry. (#D2213—50¢)

Men and Women *by Erskine Caldwell.* Caldwell's unique view of backwoods America, in twenty-two stories filled with humor, drama, and pathos. (#D2219—50¢)

CAPITOL HILL by Andrew Tully

An "inside Washington" novel, whose hero begins with dedication and ends in corruption as he jockeys for power in the tense days leading up to the National Convention.
(#T2206—75¢)

THE MANCHURIAN CANDIDATE by Richard Condon

A Korean War hero is brainwashed and made the agent of a group of political assassins. Now a movie starring Frank Sinatra, Laurence Harvey, Janet Leigh, and Angela Lansbury.
(#T1826—75¢)

THE VALLEY by Clifford Irving

A dramatic novel of conflict between father and son, set in the cattle and mining country of 19th century New Mexico.
(#P2199—60¢)

SPIRIT LAKE by MacKinlay Kantor

A vast, sweeping saga of men, women and children who lived and died for the Iowa frontier they established. By the author of *Andersonville*.
(#Q2194—95¢)

INFERNO by Robert Dundee

A convict becomes a hero during a raging forest fire, which inspires his most brutal crime—and his downfall.
(#S2159—35¢)

THE PRESENCE OF MINE ENEMIES by Turnley Walker

A searing novel that exposes the horrors of war and what it does to the men whom it forces to kill.
(#D2170—50¢)

DIAMOND HEAD by Peter Gilman

A surging novel about a dynamic family in Hawaii; now a movie starring Charlton Heston, France Nuyen, and others.
(#T1877—75¢)